Emerald Mountain

McHugh, Frances Y.

EMERALD MOUNTAIN

This Large Print Book carries the Seal of Approval of N.A.V.H.

EMERALD MOUNTAIN

FRANCES Y. McHUGH

Thorndike Press • Thorndike, Maine

Published in 1999 by arrangement with
Maureen Moran Agency.

Thorndike Large Print® Candlelight Series.

The text of this Large Print edition is unabridged.
Other aspects of the book may vary from the original edition.

Set in 16 pt. Plantin by Al Chase.

Printed in the United States on permanent paper.

Library of Congress Cataloging-in-Publication Data

McHugh, Frances Y.
Emerald Mountain / by Frances Y. McHugh.
p. cm.
ISBN 0-7862-2198-4 (lg. print : hc : alk. paper)
1. Large type books. I. Title.
[PS3563.C3685E46 1999]
813′.54—dc21 99-42432

EMERALD MOUNTAIN

Chapter One

The bus driver let me off at the foot of the mountain, took my two bags from the luggage rack and put them on the road beside me. "Someone meeting you?" he asked.

I said, "Yes."

He ducked his head toward the mountain that loomed darkly over the road. "You going up there?"

"Yes, I am."

"All alone?"

"Yes."

"It's kind of lonely up there."

"I suppose it is."

"You going to be all alone up there with Leslie Terrell?"

"Yes. I am going to work for her. I'm her new secretary." It was late afternoon, and the shadows were long on the road, but it being August, the air was still warm, even hot.

The driver got back onto the bus; then just before he slammed the door in my face he called, "It ain't a *her*. It's a *him*."

With the door closed, the huge vehicle that had brought me from Albany swooshed away, breathing deadly fumes of carbon monoxide at me from its rear end. I had to hold my breath until the fumes had been dissipated. By then the bus had disappeared around a bend in the road. When I dared to take a long breath, I said, right out loud, "And I came way up here from the city to get some fresh air!"

From behind me a man's voice said, "Plenty of fresh air up on the mountain. Let's go."

I whirled around and was face to face with a man who was at least six feet tall, with a homely yet attractive face, topped by shaggy, reddish brown hair. The eyes were a dark brown and large and had a twinkle in them.

He picked up my bags and started toward a dark green station wagon parked on the other side of the road. It may have been there when I had gotten off the bus, but I hadn't noticed it. However, considering the fact that he had my bags, I had to follow him.

He was wearing tight levis and a red plaid sports shirt open at the throat, and the rolled-up sleeves showed powerful arms dusted with reddish hairs. He slung the bags in the back of the car, opened the door to the front seat and said, "Get in."

I started to, then stopped, turned and looked up at him. The twinkle was still in his eyes. "Just a minute," I said. "Who are you?"

He grinned. "Who do you think I am? Leslie Terrell, your employer, of course."

I said, "Oh. That's what I was afraid of."

"I wrote you I'd meet you."

"That's right. You did."

"So you must be Judy Carson."

"Yes, I am." I got into the car and sat in the passenger seat, and he closed the door. Then he came around and got in behind the wheel, shut the door and started the car, making a U-turn and then heading right up the mountain road.

For a few moments I was speechless; then I said, "I expected you to be a woman."

"Why?"

"Because of your name."

"Leslie?"

"Yes."

"Sorry. It can be either male or female."

"Yes, I know."

"What difference does it make?" The car was going up and up, over a narrow dirt road and through what looked like a thick woods. The higher we got, the darker it became, until the man switched on the headlights. He said, "When I first moved up here, there wasn't even a road."

"Did you make it?"

"Yes. I rented a bulldozer and got a few men to help."

"It must have been quite a job."

"It was. But it had to be done. No one had lived up here for so long the original road had all grown over. And of course all the buildings had to be remodeled. That meant materials had to be brought up, and there had to be a road to do that."

After a few minutes we came out of the darkness of the woods, and then I could see several buildings way off in the distance and still higher up. The car swung off the narrow dirt road, which continued on, and started over the open country. I began to bounce up and down on the seat. The man turned his head and grinned at me. "Hold onto your hat," he said. Then, taking a second look, "Oh, you haven't got a hat. Well, hang onto my arm, if you want to. I can drive with one hand."

I shook my shoulder-length blonde hair back from my face and moved away from him, over closer to the car door. "I'm all right," I said, then bit my tongue as the car jounced over a hillock in the field. I decided the best thing to do was to clench my teeth; then my tongue couldn't get between them.

The man leaned across me and pushed down the button on the door. His body felt strong and muscular, and he made no effort not to lean on me. "You won't be all right if that door flies open," he said, straightening up. Then he patted my knee. "You'll get used to it," he said. "Shakes you up at first."

I didn't answer; just kept my teeth clenched.

We were nearing the buildings, and I was interested in the layout. One building was a rambling white clapboard, with gay-colored flowers up the path and all around the building. Over to one side and quite a distance behind the house was an enormous barn two stories high, of weathered brown shingles. There was an archery target fastened to one of the double barn doors. I asked, "Are you an archery fan?"

He shrugged. "I like to try my hand at it once in a while." Across a field was another house; brick, but dulled with age so the bricks were almost pink, rather than red.

My employer stopped the car in front of the white house, turned off the ignition, got out and came around to help me. As I stepped out, he said, "We'll have something to eat here at my place; then I'll take you over to your house."

"*My* house?"

"Yes. You can stay over at the brick house. I've remodeled it, and it is very comfortable. Modern conveniences and all that."

"You have electricity way up here?"

"Sure. The electric company will string up wires anywhere if you pay for them."

I was too speechless and shaken up from the wild drive across the fields to be able to comment. So he took my arm and led me up the flower-bordered path to the small square front porch. Beside it, on the right, was a large oleander shrub in a big green wooden tub; and on the left, at the foot of the two steps up to the porch, was a large bed of heavenly-smelling peppermint. As he opened the front door for me, he said, "Turn around."

I turned around and stared. Before me and spread out at the foot of the mountain was the most beautiful view I'd ever seen. Miles and miles of country stretched as far as you could see: small villages with church steeples pointing heavenward; cultivated farm land that looked like checkerboards of light and dark green; and far in the distance, another mountain which was part of a range; and sky and more sky. I had never seen so much sky. When I could speak I said, "It's beautiful. Oh, it's beautiful! I've never seen anything so lovely."

"I like it," he said, shoving me into the house. "We'll eat out on the side porch and watch the sunset."

I stood inside a room that was a combination kitchen and dining room. Over to one side was a black and very shiny old-fashioned coal stove, and in a corner was a modern electric stove. There was a large double-doored refrigerator and a pine sideboard with colorful dishes on it. The walls of the room was pine-paneled, and a round pine table stood in the middle of the room on a round braided rag rug. Around the edge of the rug could be seen wide-pegged floor boards, waxed to a dull satin sheen. Something was cooking which smelled delicious, and I discovered I was hungry. I had had a sandwich and a cup of coffee at a snack bar in Albany, where I had had to change from the New York bus and wait for two hours for the local bus. There was only one bus a day in each direction. So it had been several hours since I'd eaten. I sniffed and said, "Something smells good. What is it?"

He went over to the electric stove. "I guess you'd call it a chicken and noodle casserole. It's just one of those packaged things. I do everything the easiest way. Can you make a salad?"

"Of course."

"Good. There is a bathroom over there in the hallway. You can freshen up, if you want to, and I'll get out the things for a salad. I have everything in the refrigerator."

When I returned to the kitchen, he was gone, but all the ingredients for a salad were on the drain board of a pine cabinet-enclosed sink.

He came back just as I finished mixing the dressing and piling the assorted greens plus quartered, skinned tomatoes into a large wooden bowl. He had changed his clothes and was now wearing tan slacks and a clean white shirt. Inside the open collar of the shirt he had a blue paisley scarf. His hair was damp from a wet comb that hadn't done much to subdue the crisp waves. He said, "You're an improvement on my last secretary."

I poured some dressing on the salad and began mixing it with a wooden fork and spoon. "In what way?"

He chuckled. "She was fortyish, fat, with a grim-looking face, and was afraid of the dark."

"Did she stay over in the brick house?"

"For a while. Then she said she didn't like being over there alone."

"Oh?"

"Will that bother you?"

"I don't think so. I've never stayed in a house all alone, but I don't see why I can't. Surely there is nothing way up here to be afraid of."

"No."

"It isn't haunted or anything like that, is it?" I smiled as I said it, but a chill crept up my back, and I stopped working on the salad and crossed the fork and spoon on top of it.

He shrugged. "Oh, there's a legend that has come down through the years by word of mouth about an Indian girl by the name of Singing Bird who fell in love with a white man. I believe he was Dutch. And when her father, the chief of the tribe, found out she was pregnant, he sacrificed her to one of their gods and had his warriors kill the man. And ever since she has been supposed to roam the top of this mountain calling to her lover, whose name was Hans."

"And she is supposed to haunt the brick house?"

"So they say. That is why this entire estate has been untenanted for so long and why it was cheap enough for me to buy it."

"But why doesn't she haunt this house, too?"

"I can't imagine, unless that house was built on the spot where her lover was killed, or where she was sacrificed." Leslie took the salad bowl and carried it out to the table on the side porch that opened off the kitchen. When he came back he asked, "Do you believe in ghosts?"

"No. Do you?"

"Definitely not. They are either the figment of the imagination of a very disturbed person, or they are something faked by an unscrupulous charlatan."

I watched his face. "Then you were just trying to scare me?"

"Not at all. But I believe in being honest. Life on top of a mountain, even with modern conveniences, is at best — well, shall we say rugged?" There was a twinkle in his eyes now, and I had the feeling he was teasing me.

"In other words, you have to meet it head on?"

He gave me a quick look. "That's one way of putting it."

"Did my predecessor leave or was she fired?"

"Oh, she left voluntarily."

"Not because she was afraid to stay over in the other house alone?"

"No. As a matter of fact, when she began to complain about being over there, I moved her over here. I have three guest rooms. You can use one if you'd rather."

"No. It doesn't make any difference. Wherever you want me to stay."

"It doesn't matter, except that I like to be alone when I'm working. And if you're over at the brick house, you'll have more room to move around."

"Okay. Then shall we settle for the brick house?"

He went to the stove, took out the bubbling casserole, slipped it into a metal holder and said, "Come on." So I followed him out onto the porch. When I saw the view from there, all I could say was, "Oh!" The sky was streaked with gold, vermilion and green, and the setting sun was a large red ball. The view was the same as from the front porch, but from a different angle.

The table was set with straw place mats, and Leslie put the casserole onto the table near the salad. He seated me and sat down opposite. "You like it here?" he asked with a pleased smile.

"Oh yes! It's beautiful. I can understand why you went to all the trouble of making the road and fixing up everything. But isn't it lonely?"

He spooned some of the casserole onto a plate and handed it to me. "Help yourself to salad," he said. Then he got up. "I forgot the iced tea. It's all ready in the refrigerator. I always keep a pitcher ready. I like it better than coke or any of the other soft drinks."

He came back in a moment with a large glass pitcher of tea with tinkling ice cubes floating in it. It was on a tray together with ice-filled glasses, a plate of sliced lemon, a bowl of sugar and a tall glass of fresh mint sprigs.

"You're quite a housekeeper," I said, pouring the tea, which he had set beside me.

He grinned and resumed his seat. "I found it was easier than starving. Not much to it, really. A little common sense. No reason why an intelligent man can't whip up a meal as well as a woman. After all, the best chefs are men."

"You're right."

"But I didn't answer your question. No, it isn't lonely up here. There is always somebody coming or going, and I need a lot of time alone to do my work, both in the lab and writing."

I said, "Yes, I suppose you do."

He began to eat, and I decided I wouldn't even try to make conversation. So I just ate and enjoyed the constantly changing sunset, which was now streaks of molten gold and a purplish gray, with the sun a pale orange ball that was rapidly disappearing over the distant mountain top. In the distance there was the sound of an occasional gunshot. I asked, "What is that shooting?"

"There is a hunt club over yonder, and they sometimes have skeet shooting. That's probably what it is."

I asked, "Do you hunt?"

"No. I don't like killing things just for sport."

"Neither do I." By now the sunset was paling to a faint pink, and a cool breeze was moving the warm air. I asked, "What do you want me to do first?"

"Well, what I want you to do is correct the proofs of my last book, which have just come from my publisher. You will probably find the subject dry and uninteresting. The book is about plastics. But the next one will be more interesting."

"It will be about whatever you are working on now, I suppose."

"Yes. Crystals."

We finished our meal, and I said, "If you have anything you want to do, go on, and I will clean up."

He said, "All right. I do have something I have to do up in the lab. When you get through, go into the living room. I'll be down in a little while."

When the kitchen was tidy and all signs of

the meal out of sight, I went into the living room. It was through the narrow hallway from which the bathroom where I had freshened up opened, and it was a large, beam-ceilinged room, comfortably furnished with an assortment of masculine-type furniture. There was a large fieldstone fireplace with a jar of decorative weeds filling the opening. In a corner was a mahogany kneehole desk with two phones on it. On a coffee table was a scattering of magazines; scientific and medical journals. I wasn't interested in any of them, so I sank down on a soft tweed-covered sofa behind the coffee table and just relaxed. In the far distance I could hear the crackling of the guns shooting at the clay pigeons. The noise seemed out of place as a background to the mountain quiet. Putting my head back, I nearly fell asleep, and when Leslie said, "Okay, let's go," I jumped.

I opened my eyes and sat up. In his hand he had a package of galley proofs. "You can take these over to the other house with you and work on them in the morning. I won't need you over here until the afternoon. There is a kitchen over there, and it is completely stocked, so you can get your own breakfast."

I got to my feet and took the proofs, dimly aware that the shooting had stopped. "What about your breakfast?" I asked.

"I can take care of myself. I prefer it that way. I'm not very good at making conversation in the morning when I'm half asleep."

I couldn't help smiling. "I know what you mean. I'm that way myself. Do you want to take me over to the other house now?"

"Yes. I'll drive you over. Your bags are still in the car."

"Is there a road?"

"There is, but I usually just go over the fields. It's shorter."

I decided to play it by ear and take things as they came, so I got into the car and let him drive me over to the other house. The sun had disappeared behind a distant mountain, and it was getting dark. Then in a few minutes it *was* dark, and there wasn't a light in sight except one Leslie had left on in his living room. That is, there weren't any lights on the mountain. In the distance there were the lights of the villages that made up part of the view, and a low-hanging new moon just coming over the horizon opposite the one where the sun had set. Leslie said, "That moon reminds me of an Indian legend that one of the old natives told me. He said his grandmother told it to him when he was a boy. It was about an aged squaw who was supposed to have charge of the doors of day and night; to open and close them at the proper time. She also hung up the new moon in the skies, and cut up the old one for stars."

"What a charming story. I like it better than what we now know about the moon."

"I'm inclined to agree with you. At least it makes less demands on us poor mortals here on this planet."

As we neared the brick house, he said, "I think you will be comfortable here. If there is anything you need you can call me. There is a house-to-house telephone in each apartment, as well as an outside one."

I said, "I'm sure I'll be all right."

When we went into the house, he snapped on lights all over the place; ceiling lights and lamps and a few wall lights. It immediately dispersed the gloom, which otherwise might have overwhelmed me. He brought in my bags and set them in the front entrance hall, where there was a deacon's bench and a console table. Beneath one arm he had the galley proofs. He tossed them onto the table, saying, "There are two complete apartments here. You can have your choice, but I'd recommend the one here on the first floor."

He began showing me around. There was a coat closet in the entrance hall, and he opened the door to show me the interior. It was empty except for a bag of golf clubs. Then we went into a large wood-paneled living room, furnished with comfortable if inexpensive furniture, with the exception of a tall inlaid cabinet that was the most beautiful thing I had ever seen. I went over to examine it more closely. "This is beautiful," I said, passing a hand lightly over the inlay on the doors at the front.

"I bought it from a missionary who brought it back from Indo-China. He and his wife and son stayed here for a while this spring. Let me show you." He came over and opened the double doors. Inside were a series of various-sized drawers, some open, some with doors of their own, some with lids that would open only when the drawer was pulled out.

"It's fascinating," I said. "I should think you would have it over in the house you live in."

He closed the doors, and we moved away. "The Heaths had this apartment. When they left, they offered to sell me some of the things they had brought home from the East. They needed some quick money. I hope to sell everything at a profit eventually, so there is no use moving any of it."

"There is more?"

"Yes. This inlaid coffee table and this Buddha." He led me to a side table on which was a green bronze Buddha about twenty inches high. It was a new conception of a Buddha to me. To begin with, it was female. It was sitting cross-legged with folded hands, and on the head was a sort of cap with an ornament that went up to a tall spire, like a church steeple.

He said, "It is called Yaksa. She is the Buddha of Fertility. The story goes that girls unable to have children prayed to her and brought her gifts, and those she favored were in time blessed with offspring."

"Which they probably would have had anyway."

He smiled. "Don't tell me you're a skeptic."

"Let's just say I'm practical, or is the word realistic? Besides, I thought there was only one Buddha; the fat one that sits in Kamakura, Japan. I believe they call it Daibutsee, or Great Buddha."

"Oh no. There have been many Buddhas. A Buddha was one of a series of teachers who brought enlightenment to man. The one in Kamakura was the last one. His name was Gautara."

"I wonder what he is doing in Japan. I thought Buddhism originated in India."

"It did. But later it spread to China, Burma, Japan, Tibet and parts of southwest Asia."

"How interesting. This one has jewels for eyes: emeralds. Are they real?"

"Oh yes. And quite valuable, as a matter of fact. Oriental emeralds are very rare and precious. Come; I'll show you the rest of the place."

I followed him around the first floor. There was a small but adequate modern kitchen; the refrigerator and pantry were completely stocked. A door from the kitchen led out to a back porch, and beyond this was a garden that sloped down the mountainside. Across a small hall out of the living room there were two bedrooms, connected by a bath. One bedroom was a soft rose and white, the other apple green and jonquil yellow. The bathroom was tiled in a light brown with a turquoise tub, basin and john. Turquoise towels hung on the racks. "You have good taste," I told him. "This is all very attractive."

He said, "I'm glad you like it. Now come upstairs and see the other apartment."

"This is fine," I said. "And I'd rather be on the first floor."

"Look at the upstairs place, anyway. Then you won't be wondering what is up there in case you hear unfamiliar sounds in the night."

Deciding I'd better not ask what he meant by that, I followed him back to the front entrance hall and up a flight of stairs that led to the second floor. It was all open, and there seemed no way of closing off the first floor from the second. Nor were there doors to any of the rooms in either apartment except the bathrooms. I knew I wouldn't like this if I were living there permanently and someone else were living upstairs. But I was to have the entire house to myself, so it didn't matter.

The second floor apartment was a duplicate of the one downstairs except that there was nothing in it from Indo-China, and the colors were different. The upstairs bedrooms were pale blue and white and lavender and gray. The bathroom was black and white with bright red towels.

We wandered through the rooms, which rambled into one another like a big spacious barn. The whole place was comfortable and charming, but there was no privacy. I said, "I still would rather be downstairs."

"I thought you would." He opened a door to an ascending stairway. "These go up to an unfinished attic. Some day I'll make it into a small apartment." He closed the door and walked over to the main staircase, and I followed him down to the first floor.

In the downstairs living room was a large table-like desk between two windows. The upstairs didn't have anything like it. There were two phones on it; one was brown, the other black. Leslie said, "The brown phone connects with my house. If you want me, just pick up the receiver and press this button." He touched a button beneath the dial.

I said, "All right."

"The black phone is for outside calls. The upstairs apartment has its own phones. If you have to make any outside calls, I would appreciate it if you would keep a record of them so I can check the bill."

"I doubt if I'll have any occasion to call outside, unless it is for you."

He turned and looked at me. "Why did you accept a job like this?"

He took me by surprise, and for a moment I didn't know what to say. Then I decided the truth was the simplest way out. "Well, I had come to — I guess you would call it a dead end. And then I saw the ad for this job and decided it was just what I needed. I was a good stenographer, and I wanted to get out of the city and away from everything, if you know what I mean?"

He scrutinized my face until I became embarrassed; then he asked, "An unsatisfactory love affair?"

I turned away and picked up the smaller of my bags. "That was part of it," I said.

He picked up the larger bag. "Which bedroom do you want this in?" he asked.

"The rose and white one, please." It was the larger of the two, and a corner room with double windows on two sides.

He followed me into the large square room, which had an old-fashioned double brass bed with a snowy white chenille hobnail bedspread. The floor was wide-pegged boards with hooked scatter rugs in strategic places around the room. There was an old-fashioned rocking chair, a table with a lamp on it and a couple of *Life* magazines, and beside the bed was a small table with a reading lamp and a clock radio. A bureau with a large mirror stood between the two windows that faced the back garden, and in a corner was a luggage stand. Leslie put the bag on the stand so I could open it easily. "There, I guess you are all set now." He turned to me and smiled. The look of scrutiny was gone. Now he was just being the gracious host. "Sleep well. I'll phone you early in the afternoon, and we'll go over those proofs together."

I said, "All right. And thank you."

He bowed. "My pleasure. Good night."

"Good night." He went out and left the house, and I was alone.

Suddenly I had the feeling that someone was watching me. I whirled around and looked into the living room, but there was no one there. It was only Yaksa, the Buddha of Fertility, staring at me with her emerald eyes. The light from a table lamp shone on them and made them appear to be winking at me. I went into the living room, snapped off all the lights, turned off the hall light and the one on the porch. As I did so, I heard Leslie's car drive away. I locked the front door.

Returning to the bedroom, I undressed, took a leisurely bath — there was plenty of hot water — and got into bed. When I'd finished my bath, I had noticed the lights were on over in the white house, both on the first and second floors. Well, why not? It was only nine-thirty, although it seemed much later to me because I had had a long day and I was very tired. The trip up from the city had been exhausting, and I was too sleepy to read or even glance at a magazine. So I put out my lights, got into bed and went to sleep.

It must have been about three o'clock

when something awakened me. The room was very dark, and for a moment I lay listening. There wasn't a sound. Then what had aroused me? And why was my heart pounding so hard? Then I heard what sounded like a woman crying. I sat up in bed, listening. There it was again, low, stifled sobbing. And it seemed to be coming from the living room. I jumped out of bed, my feet fumbling for my slippers. I didn't wait to put on a robe, but hurried out of the bedroom and into the living room. At first I thought I saw a white vaporish figure floating across the room. Was it Singing Bird? I asked, "Who's there?" But no one answered me, and the white figure disappeared. I felt my way to a lamp and snapped it on. There was no one in the room. And Yaksa sat on the table with her enigmatic look, her Oriental emerald eyes reflecting the light from the lamp. Everything was quiet now, and I snapped off the light and started back to the bedroom. Then I heard the soft crying again. This time it was coming from upstairs. Dared I go up? I had to. Going out to the foyer, I snapped on the light at the foot of the stairs and started up.

I searched the place thoroughly but could find nothing, so I went back downstairs, reaching the foyer just as the front door was closing. It had been locked, so how could it have gotten open far enough to be closing now — unless someone had been in the house when I had locked the door? I went over to it, opened it all the way and looked out. In the darkness I could see no one. I called, "Hello? Is anyone there?" No one answered me, so I closed the door, locked it again, and went back to bed. But I didn't sleep much for the rest of the night.

Chapter Two

The next morning I was sitting at the table-desk proofreading the galleys when an ear-splitting noise shattered the peacefulness of the mountaintop. Jumping up, I hurried out to the front porch just as a motorcycle zoomed up the road. There were two people on it, but I couldn't determine their sex because of their helmets, pants and black leather jackets. The one on the rumble seat, or whatever they call it on a motorcycle, had a guitar slung over his or her back. The motorcycle swung around with a flourish and stopped at the foot of the porch steps. The two people got down and pulled off their helmets, and I was able to see that one was a man and one was a girl.

The man parked the motorcycle at the side of the steps, and the girl said, "Hi. We're Gail and Roger Ferguson. We're going to be in the upstairs apartment for a while."

I had all I could do to keep from saying, "Oh no!" But of course I had no right to protest. The house wasn't mine; I was just an employee of the owner. So I said, "Oh?

Well, come in. I'm Judy Carson. I am Mr. Terrell's secretary."

Gail said, "Yes, we know. We have just been over there." She had long straight blonde hair, lighter than mine, parted in the middle and falling over her shoulders halfway to her waist. She adjusted the strap of her guitar so it was more comfortable across her slim shoulders, turned and looked at the view. The fact that she was attracted to it made me like her and feel that somewhere under the outer trappings there was a soul.

The boy, Roger, had curly brown hair, long enough to be called a bob. It was parted on the side and hung around his neck in a very untidy manner. He was tall and lank and looked as if a good bath would improve him. When he finished parking the motorcycle so it was standing securely and turned toward me, I saw his eyes were a light blue, and he looked everywhere but directly at me. It gave me a queer, uneasy feeling.

I said, "Please come in, and I'll take you upstairs."

They followed me into the house. But in the entrance hall Gail said, "We know our way around. We've been here before," and ran up the stairs. Roger followed her, and I just stood staring at their legs and feet as they went upward. Who were they? And why were they there? And why hadn't Leslie Terrell told me they were coming?

I went back to my proofreading but couldn't keep my mind on it. Such terms as plastisol slush-molding techniques and hetron-type endochloro polyester resins made no sense at all to me.

Overhead it was very quiet. No footsteps, no voices. What were they doing that they were so quiet? Making love? Were they man and wife or brother and sister? And what were they to Leslie Terrell? I thought of calling him and asking, but if he was working in his laboratory I didn't want to disturb him. He'd said he would call me early in the afternoon. I'd better wait.

At lunch time I fixed myself a salad and iced tea from the supplies in my kitchen. There was a heavenly odor of flowers coming through the screen door, but the sun was hot, and bees buzzed around, waiting for me to open the door. I wondered if I should call Gail and Roger and offer them some lunch. Then I decided they would probably prefer to be left alone. And I knew their kitchen was as well stocked as mine.

After a while I heard footsteps overhead,

then the sound of the guitar, and the girl and the man began to sing a rock and roll folk song. Were they entertainers? Maybe I should know who they were, although I didn't pay much attention to that kind of program on TV, nor did I ever buy records of that type. But they sounded very professional.

By the time the phone rang I had finished lunch, had the dishes washed and put away and had read about one third of the galleys. Leslie said, "Good morning. Or I guess it's afternoon. Did you sleep well?"

"Very well, thank you. And I've read some of the galleys." Somehow I didn't like to tell him about what I'd thought I'd heard and seen during the night.

He said, "Good. I'll come over for you in a few minutes. I hope Gail and Roger won't bother you. If they do, let me know. Gail is my cousin and likes to come up here, as she expresses it, to get away from it all."

I didn't say anything, so he went on, "Well, see you in a few minutes. Bring the galleys with you. And in that table-desk in the living room, you'll find a stenographer's notebook. Bring that along. I have some letters to dictate."

I replaced the phone and gathered up the galleys, keeping the ones I'd read separate from those I hadn't, found the notebook that had been half used, and put an elastic band around it all. Then I took a handful of pencils and was ready. But when Leslie's car drove up to the front porch, Gail came tumbling down the stairs and almost knocked me over in the entrance hall by pushing ahead of me to get out of the door. As soon as Leslie stepped from his car, she flung herself at him and hugged him. Over her shoulder he grinned at me, kissed her cheek and broke the strangle hold she had around his neck.

Roger came out of the house and shook hands with Leslie. "Nice of you to let us come," he said.

Leslie said, "Always glad to have you." Then he came over to me. "Ready?" he asked.

I said, "Yes."

He said, "Okay. Come on," took my arm and put me into the car.

Gail asked, "Can we come too?"

He turned, and I thought he seemed annoyed. "No. We are going to work. You stay here."

The girl looked disappointed, turned and walked away toward the back gardens. In the car, bumping across the fields to the white house, Leslie said, "She's a nice kid, but she's a little far out."

I asked, "Is Roger her brother or her husband?"

"Her husband." The way he snapped out the words silenced me, and I didn't ask any more questions.

We worked out on the side porch all afternoon, reading the galleys together, discussing a possible rearrangement of chapters. Then he dictated a few letters which were so technical I didn't understand a word of them.

He was completely impersonal with me, and I found myself experiencing a growing respect for him. For a man so young — he couldn't have been more than twenty-seven or twenty-eight — he had a great deal of poise and a quiet strength that intrigued me.

When we finished working, he brought out a couple of glasses of iced tea, and we sat and chatted like old friends about nothing in particular. He asked me again why I had come way up on the mountain to work for him, and I repeated what I'd told him the previous evening. Then I asked him, "Do you live up here the year around?"

He said, "No. I have an apartment down in the city on East Thirty-fifth Street near the East River, but I come up here as much as I can. I can write in the apartment, but when I have lab work to do I have to come up here."

I wanted to ask him if he was married, then decided not to. It really wasn't any of my business. But then, neither was it his business why I had accepted his job.

While we were drinking our iced tea and chatting, Gail arrived. She'd walked over the fields. She looked hot, and her hair was wet with perspiration around her flushed face. She had discarded the leather jacket but was wearing the same black pants with a white cotton knit turtleneck shirt like Roger's with several strings of love beads around her neck. She said, "Hi. May I join you now?" and sank down on a chair near us.

Les said, "Yes, we're through working. I'll get you a glass of iced tea." He went into the kitchen, and Gail looked over at me. "You going to be here long?" she asked.

"What do you mean?" Instinctively I resented the girl. She was too cool, too arrogant, too possessive of my boss. And yet that wasn't strictly true, either. Nothing she had done or said, actually, gave me any reason to jump to that conclusion.

Before I answered her, Les returned with a tall glass of iced tea and gave it to her. As he sat down, he asked, "How's it going?"

She sipped the tea and shrugged. "So so. We're doing another album."

Les said, "Good. The others selling well?"

"Well enough, if Roger didn't mistake the money for which we have to work for pennies from heaven."

Les gazed out over the landscape thoughtfully. "Anything I can do?" he asked.

She gulped some more iced tea. "Nothing, thanks. I'm a big girl now, and I tell myself I got myself into it against everybody's advice, so I can jolly well get myself out."

"Do you want out?" Les brought his gaze back from the distant landscape and focused it on her face.

She looked down into the glass of tea and moved the glass so the ice in it tinkled. "I don't know," she said. "Sometimes I do and sometimes I don't. I think sometimes I'd like to lead a bourgeois type of life, dike Mother and Dad. You know, have a home and kids."

"Maybe you will some day."

"Not with Roger. He thinks that kind of life is — well, stagnation or a slow death. Besides, the last doctor I went to told me I can't have children." She smiled with one side of her mouth. "I've even tried praying to Yaksa." Then she glanced up at him. "Why did you have to be my cousin?" she asked.

He frowned. "Don't start that again," he said.

She sighed. "Sorry."

I was beginning to feel uncomfortable. I'd finished my glass of tea, and I put it on the table, saying, "Perhaps I'd better mosey over to the other house. I can walk over. It will do me good."

But Leslie jumped up. "No, I'll drive you over. And you too, Gail. Come on."

Gail pouted. "Can't I stay? I'll get your dinner for you." Her large greenish-blue eyes pleaded like those of a child wanting a lollipop. I noticed her eyes were her best feature. Her nose was small and pert, her mouth large and nicely shaped, but with a droop at the corners. Her eyes were large and luminous, and she had them very cleverly made up. In answer to her question, Les asked, "What about Roger?"

"So? What about him?"

"Won't he be expecting you back?"

She smiled and tossed me a challenging glance. "*She* can take care of him," she said. Then to me, "I'm sure you wouldn't mind. He is real good fun when he wants to be.

And I'm not the jealous kind."

I turned on her, furious now. "Thanks, but no thanks," I said. "I'm not in the habit of taking care of other girls' husbands."

Leslie said, "On second thought, Judy, I have some more letters I'd like to dictate. You'd better stay. And, Gail, you run on back to the brick house and get your husband's dinner. You'll find a steak in the freezer. I'll drive Judy back later."

"But *I* have to walk?"

"Why not? You're young, strong and probably need the exercise."

"Okay." She thought a moment. "Can I get myself a little more iced tea first? It's going to be a hot walk."

Les said, "Sure. There is a glass pitcher of it in the refrigerator. Help yourself."

When she left us, he said to me, "I'm sorry you had to be subjected to this. She's really a good kid but, as I say, a little far out."

She was in the house for quite a while, and I could tell Les was getting nervous about it. He said, "I wonder what she's doing."

"Maybe she wanted to wash her hands or something, before she started back."

He relaxed a little. "Maybe," he said.

When she came out, she said, "Thanks for the iced tea. But I don't think you're very sociable. Or is the word hospitable?"

Leslie grinned. "You should know me well enough to be used to that."

She toyed with one of the strings of love beads she was wearing around her neck. "You used to be more friendly," she said, and I thought she was close to tears.

"That was when we were kids and I didn't know any better."

"You mean that was before the family began to make a stink about it."

Leslie's face flushed, and he avoided meeting my eyes. "Well, yes. After all, you were an attractive girl, and I had never seen many white girls. Where we were stationed in Indo-China, the few white women, missionaries and teachers and a few nurses, were all older than I and not too physically attractive. God bless them."

A dreamy look came into Gail's eyes. "And I had never seen you; just pictures. The first time I saw you, in our living room in Westport, I flipped. I remember I came in from high school and there you were: tall, tanned, with that bright red hair — any girl's dream man. And to me you were a man then. You were going on seventeen, and I was only sixteen less a month."

So he had been to Indo-China, had he? Did that explain the Buddha and the other things? Was there more of it than he had told me?

Gail sighed, gave me a dirty look and said, "Oh, well, water over the dam."

Leslie said, "Exactly." Then, in a brighter tone of voice, "Now scoot. Judy and I have more work to do."

Without looking at either of us again, she walked into the house, through the kitchen and out the front door, and in a few minutes we could see her trudging across the fields in the hot sun. I felt sorry for her and said, "Weren't you a little hard on her? After all, it is pretty hot."

His lips tightened. "If I hadn't been hard on her, I'd never have gotten her out of here. She's having one of her fits."

"What do you mean by that?"

"Oh, she gets spells when she feels sorry for herself, and she really hasn't anything to justify it. Anything that's wrong she's brought upon herself."

"Don't we all?"

He shrugged. "Sometimes yes, sometimes no."

I began to wonder if I would ever get to know this man. He seemed to have many sides; some nice, some difficult to understand.

He said, "I guess our conversation

sounded rather strange to you."

I shrugged. "It's none of my business. I'm here to do your secretarial work. Your former life is of no interest to me."

He thought that over for a moment, then said, "No, I suppose not. But I feel I owe you some kind of an explanation. You see, my mother and father were missionaries. They were stationed in a small village in Indo-China for years. I was born there and lived there until I was sixteen. There was an American school near us where I went until I was ten. Then my parents were killed in a native uprising, and a couple of their friends, also missionaries, who had a son about my age, fled with me to another village. They established a mission there and cared for me and taught me and Joshua until we were sixteen. Then they decided I'd better come to the states and have proper schooling. I hated to leave them and Josh, but nevertheless I was shipped over to Aunt Margaret and Uncle Jim, whom I'd never seen. I stayed with them in Westport for a few months, going to high school with Gail." He hesitated. "That was when we got to like each other."

He swirled the ice around in his glass. "I guess I went a little overboard for her, not having seen any pretty white girls over in

Indo-China. So Aunt Margaret and Uncle Jim decided it would be a good idea if I went away to school. They sent me to a boys' boarding school in Massachusetts. My parents had left enough money for my education; money they'd inherited from relatives." He sighed. "Well, after that I went on to M.I.T. and got my B.S. and a job with a pharmaceutical company. Stayed there for a couple of years, then wrote a book about what it was like to be a child in Indo-China, made enough money to buy this place and decided to try it on my own." He shrugged. "And so here I am."

I didn't remember the book, so decided not to comment on it. I said, "Did you and Gail see much of each other after you went away to school?"

"No, not really. Summers I got jobs and visited friends I'd met in school and college. Then Gail left home and moved down to the Village. She'd graduated from high school and went for two years to a junior college where she majored in music. Then she met Roger in the Village, and a couple of years ago they got married. Lately they've been coming up here from time to time."

"And you never married?"

"No. After Gail and I were separated, I lost interest in girls. I threw myself into my studies, and since college I've been too busy." He gazed out over the distant landscape for a moment, then said, "What about some dinner? You'd better eat here with me."

I said, "All right," and we both got up and went into the kitchen. Opening the refrigerator door, he took out the pitcher of iced tea, now only half full. Then he looked down into it, swirled it around, got a spoon and took out what looked like crushed mint leaves. "Now how did that get in there?" He smelled of the tiny green stuff grouped in a bunch on the wet spoon, then emptied the entire pitcher into the sink. There was a grim look on his face. I asked, "Why did you do that?"

He began to wash the pitcher vigorously under running hot water. He didn't answer me.

I asked again, "Why did you do that — dump the whole pitcher of tea?"

Without looking at me, he said, "I didn't like the looks of it."

"The green stuff — wasn't it only crushed mint leaves?"

"No. It was crushed oleander leaves."

I said, "So?"

He looked at me then, and his eyes were angry. "So? Oleander is poisonous. It has the properties of digitalis. I don't know whether taking it that way would hurt us or not, but I'd rather not take chances."

I gasped. "Oh! But who would put anything like that in the tea, here in your house?"

He didn't answer; just took a towel and began drying the pitcher.

"Gail?" I asked.

His mouth tightened. "Certainly not."

"If she did, she probably doesn't know oleander is poisonous."

He said, "No. Probably not." But he didn't sound at all convinced, and he didn't suggest making fresh tea for dinner.

There were some cold cuts and potato salad in the refrigerator, I made a tossed salad, and we had coffee and ice cream for dessert.

We didn't talk much as we ate out on the side porch, as we had the night before. Even the sunset wasn't pretty, as it had been the previous evening. But at least there were no sounds of shooting coming across the valley from the Hunt Club.

After we'd finished eating, we cleared the table and washed and dried the dishes together, still not having much to say. When I asked, "What about those additional letters you wanted to dictate to me?" he said,

"There aren't any. That was just an excuse to keep you and Gail apart. But I guess it's all right for you to go back to the brick house now. She and Roger are probably having their dinner up in their apartment and won't bother you. You may hear them rehearsing, but you'll enjoy that. They really are good."

"Yes, I heard them this afternoon just before you came over for me."

Riding across the fields to the brick house, we heard thunder rumbling in the distance. Les said, "Guess we're in for a storm. They come up quickly here in the mountains." Then he added, "And that reminds me of another story about the old squaw who used to hang up the moon. It was reported that when she was in an angry mood, she darkened the sky and sent torrents of rain over the hills."

"Well, if she'll cool things off a little, I won't mind."

"Nor I." Then he said, "Don't let Gail bug you. If she gives you any trouble, let me know. I'm sorry you have to have them in the house, but they usually don't stay long."

He was right. When we reached the brick house, the motorcycle was gone. Frowning, Les came into the house with me and called, "Gail? Roger?"

There was no answer, and he ran up the

stairs. I listened, but I couldn't hear any voices; just his footsteps stamping across the floor. In a few moments he came down, crumpling a piece of paper in one hand. "They're gone," he said, and tossed the crumpled paper on the side table.

"But they just got here."

"I know. That's the way they are." He stood thinking a moment, then said, "See you," strode out of the house, got into his car and drove off. I couldn't resist picking up the piece of crumpled paper he'd thrown onto the table. On it was scrawled:

"We're up, up, up and away. We love you."

"Love, love, love is the only thing."

I threw the paper back on the table, muttering, "Hippie stuff."

Feeling deflated, I wandered into the living room to put the galleys and the stenographic notebook on the table-desk. The sky was darkening, and the rumbles of thunder were coming closer. Inadvertently I glanced over at Yaksa to see if her green eyes were watching me. They were gone!

With a little cry I ran over to the statue for a closer look. It must be a trick of the rapidly fading light. The sky was quickly darkening, and there was an occasional flash of lightning. When I reached the statue, I saw for a certainty that the two emerald eyes were gone. The statue was staring at me with blinded eyes. To be sure, I touched the empty sockets. They were without a doubt empty. I snapped on all of the lights and searched the table on which the statue stood. And I searched the floor all around. Perhaps the stones hadn't been fastened in tightly enough and had fallen out. But they were not anywhere to be found.

So now what should I do? Call Leslie, of course. I went to the desk and used the house to house phone. When he answered, I said, "Something peculiar has happened."

"What?"

"The Buddha's eyes are gone."

"Are you sure?"

"Of course. And I've looked all around for them. But if they'd accidentally fallen out, they would be around somewhere on the table or the floor. They're not."

There was silence on the other end of the phone, and I waited. Then I asked, "Hadn't you better call the police?"

"No. And don't you. Just don't worry about it."

"But do you think Gail and Roger — ?"

"No! Just forget it!" The phone clicked in my ear, and the line was dead.

Well, if he felt that way about it —

The storm broke with a deluge of rain, blinding flashes of lightning and heavy rolls of thunder which was too close for comfort. I have never been frightened of thunderstorms, but this was worse than any I'd ever experienced. The lightning actually crackled and one time came down like a big ball of fire into the road in front of the house. Then the lights went out, and I was in pitch darkness. I didn't have a flashlight, and I hadn't noticed any candles or matches anywhere in the house, so there was nothing for me to do but feel my way to a chair in the living room and sit down and wait until the storm passed. There were no lights over in the white house, either, so the electricity must have been put out of commission there also. I tried both phones. They were both dead.

It was the first time in my life I had ever been entirely alone without human contact of some kind. I knew there was nothing to be frightened of, but I *was* frightened. To tell the truth, I didn't feel that I was really all alone. I could feel a presence near me. I asked, "Is anybody here?" I imagined I heard breathing, but no one answered me. There was another flash of lightning, and I thought I saw a shadowy form over by the Buddha. Then I saw a hand with fingers glowing like ghostly talons of red, green and blue. It was reaching out toward the Buddha. I was so frightened I couldn't move. After a moment I asked, "Who are you?" My voice sounded strange and as if it came from an echo chamber. There was no answer, but the hand disappeared. Then something cold and wet brushed across my cheek, and that was all I remembered until I felt myself being lifted. I opened my eyes. The lights were on, and I was in Leslie's arms, being carried over to the sofa. "What happened?" I asked.

"You tell *me*. I came over to bring you some candles and found you on the floor." He laid me down on the sofa and stood looking at me. I managed to sit up and glance around. There was no one over by the Buddha and no one in the room but Leslie and me. I said, "The lights went out. And I didn't have a flashlight or anything. Then I had the feeling that someone was here in the room with me, and one time when the lightning flashed I thought I saw a shadowy form over by the Buddha. Then I saw —" I shuddered and began to tremble — "I saw a hand over by the Buddha. It was ghostly and it glowed. It was sort of skeletal and radiated colors: green and red and blue."

He sat down beside me and put an arm around me. It was comforting to have him close beside me, and I found my head resting on his broad shoulder. After a moment he said, "You'd better come over and stay at my place."

I pulled myself away from him and, with a desperate effort, got myself under control. "No," I said, "I'll be all right here, now the lights are on. It was just the storm."

He got to his feet. "I'll take a look around." He went over to the Buddha, felt the empty eye sockets, stood looking down at the statue for a moment, then turned away from it and said, "I'll go take a look upstairs."

While he was up there, I got up and looked all around the first floor. There were no signs of anyone having been there, but when I caught sight of my face in a mirror I almost shrieked. Where the cold wet thing had touched my cheek there were black streaks. Why hadn't Leslie mentioned them? He must have seen them.

He was upstairs for quite a while, and I had time to clean my face before he came down. Perhaps I should have spoken to him about the black marks on my face, but I didn't. There was no doubt there was something strange happening on top of the mountain, but if he didn't want to tell me — okay.

If I'd been smart, I would have resigned right then and there and asked him to take me down to the village. There was a hotel over in Cobleskill where I could have spent the night. But when my employer came downstairs, all I said was, "Will the lights be all right now?"

I thought he looked worried, and for a moment he seemed to be going to tell me something, but changed his mind. "Yes," he said, "the lights should be all right now, barring another storm. It was probably something at the power plant."

I said, "Well, thank you for coming over with the candles. I'll put them in the bedroom where I can find them easily if I should need them in the night."

He stood looking at me for a moment; then he said, "Sure you don't want to move over to my place?"

I said, "No. But thank you anyway."

He turned and went out, and I heard the car drive away.

I stood in the entrance hall, wondering what to do. It was too early to go to bed, and I didn't feel like working or reacting. Then I decided I'd go upstairs and have a look around myself. I snapped on the switch at the foot of the stairs that lighted the upper hall and went slowly up the stairs. Up there, I snapped on lights in the rooms as I went along. If Leslie was watching, he would see the lights and wonder what I was doing. Or maybe he would guess I was just satisfying my woman's curiosity. Would he call it snooping? It wasn't really. Not from my point of view. I just wanted to be sure no one was up there.

I had just about decided there wasn't when something crashed down on my head from behind, and instantly everything went black. The next thing I knew I was lying out on the lawn in front of the house, looking up at the stars, which must have come out as soon as the storm was over. I felt of my head. There was a lump on the back of it as large as half a baseball, and it was sore when I touched it. And the grass was wet. My back was wet and chilled, but it was a while before I could move, I was so stunned. Finally I was able to sit up and look around. The house was all dark. I got to my feet and tottered over to the porch, up the two steps and over to the front door. It wouldn't open. I banged on it and rattler the knob. It wouldn't budge. Could I climb in a window? I found I couldn't. With the exception of those on either side of the porch, they were all too high off the ground. Besides, they were screened with full screens that hooked from the inside; the kind that are interchangeable with storm windows for the winter. And I had nothing with which to cut a hole in a screen. I felt my way around to the kitchen door. It wouldn't open, yet I knew I hadn't locked it or hooked the screen door. Returning to the front, I looked over at the white house. There were lights in a room on the second floor. Was that the laboratory? And could I walk over the fields in the dark? I remembered the bumps and ruts the car had gone over when Leslie had driven me last evening and early this evening. In the dark I would probably trip over them, and if I fell and broke a leg I'd have to lie there all night. I didn't like the prospect. But I had to try — or sit on the porch all night. Who, I wondered, had put out all the lights in the house? The last I remembered they had all been on in both apartments.

I started toward the white house, stepping very carefully so I wouldn't fall. I'd gotten about halfway there when the light in the house went out, which probably meant Leslie had gone to bed. I stopped walking and looked around. There was now nothing to see but the stars overhead. There wasn't even a moon; just the kind of a night I usually liked, a black sky with millions and trillions of stars. Something slithered past my ankles, and I jumped and cried out. What was it? I wasn't familiar with nocturnal animals that inhabited a mountain top. Was it a rat, a snake, a rabbit, a skunk? It could be one of many things. I started to walk on, then realized I'd lost my bearings. While looking around me, I'd turned, and in the darkness I couldn't see either of the houses. And being a city girl I wasn't familiar enough with the stars to be able to chart my course by them. Suppose I went in the wrong direction and got lost? I could easily get into the woods, and then I'd be out of luck for sure.

I leaned over and felt of the ground upon which I was standing. It was level but damp from the rain, so I didn't want to sit on it, especially when I didn't know what kind of creatures were slithering around on it.

Then, gradually, my eyes became accustomed to the darkness and I could see the outline of the white house against the starlit sky. With a sigh of relief I began walking toward it. The lump on my head was aching, and my knees seemed to want to buckle, but I wouldn't let them. And now it was beginning to get chilly; even cold. Naturally, it would be cooler up here on the mountain than down in the valley.

Determinedly I staggered along until I was close enough to the house to be able to see it better. Would Leslie be angry at me for waking him up? For surely by now he must be asleep. And he'd probably scold me for not coming over with him when he'd suggested it. I sighed. Oh, well, it couldn't be helped.

When I reached the house I was at the back of it. I walked around to the front and knocked on the door, waited, then knocked again. I called, "Mr. Terrell, it's Judy Carson." There wasn't a sound. I was shivering now from the cold and feeling very near tears. Then I began to pound on the door with both fists. Finally Leslie called from an upper window, "What's the matter? Who is it?"

"It's Judy Carson. Please let me in."

"Wait a minute. I'll be right down."

In a moment I heard his footsteps coming down the stairs. Then the light flashed on, the door opened, and I was facing a very sleepy-looking Leslie Terrell in blue and white-striped pajamas with attractively rumpled hair.

I stumbled into the hall and into his arms. Then I was crying, and he was holding me close to him and saying, "There, there, don't cry. Tell me what happened."

With an arm around me, he led me into the living room and over to the sofa. It was several minutes before I could get myself under control enough to tell him what had happened to me after he'd left the brick house. When I finished he said, "Well, let's not worry about it now. Come upstairs, and I'll put you in one of the guest rooms for the rest of the night. We'll talk about it in the morning."

I followed him upstairs, and he got me a pair of his pajamas and turned down the bedcovers. "I'll go over for your things in the morning," he said.

I just nodded, and he left me and closed the door. I saw there was a key on the inside, and I turned it, got out of my wet clothes and into the pajamas, the legs and arms of which I had to roll up. Then I got into the maple spool bed, which looked very inviting and was as comfortable as it looked.

Chapter Three

I slept fitfully, and in the morning when I heard Leslie moving around and going downstairs, I didn't know what to do about breakfast. He had told me he preferred to breakfast alone, so I decided to keep away until he'd finished. Then I could go down and get myself something. I found a well equipped bathroom along the hall not far from my room, and on the hand basin were several fresh towels which I presumed were for me. The bathroom was steamy from Leslie's shower, but I fanned the door a few times, and the steam was quickly dissipated.

I had just finished dressing when he called me. "Miss Carson! Judy!"

I opened my door. "Yes?"

"Hurry up. Breakfast is ready!"

"Oh? Well, I'll be right down."

I had no choice but to wear the same clothes I'd had on yesterday. My dress, a tailored shirtwaist dress of drip-dry and wrinkle-resistant fabric in a soft blue, was still all right in spite of the soaking the back of it had gotten while I was lying unconscious on the wet grass.

When I went into the kitchen, breakfast was on the round pine table. There was orange juice, I presumed frozen, bacon and eggs, toast and coffee. I said, “I wasn’t going to bother you at breakfast time.”

He grinned. “Sit down,” he ordered, and poured my coffee.

I sat down, and he sat opposite me. I began to eat silently. Unfortunately, I was very conscious of him across the table from me. He had on a white lab suit and looked like a hospital intern. After a while he said, “Would you like to learn something about what I do in the lab?”

I said, “If you want me to.”

“It would help you to know what I am writing about.” Our eyes met, and a flash of — I don’t know what to call it — understanding, rapport, electricity, vibrations, passed between us. Whatever it was, it suddenly made me feel as if I *belonged* somewhere for the first time since Mom and Dad had died, and I was almost happy again.

Perhaps this is a good time to tell you why I happened to come up to this lonely mountain top to work and live with a complete stranger. It began about a year ago when I lost both my parents in a plane crash. They’d been out to the coast, where my father, who was an executive for a wholesale paper company, had some business. Mother had gone along to attend a dinner that was to be given in his honor. On the way home, in a company plane, they ran into a storm and crashed.

We had been living in Hartsdale, where I had grown up. I was an only child, and the three of us were very close until I went to college. Then I was away for the four years it took me to get a B.A. in English at Cornell University. It was at Cornell I met Randy Winthrop and became engaged to him. We had never met before we went to college, although he lived in Scarsdale, the next town to Hartsdale in Westchester County. We had planned on a late June wedding, which would have been after graduation. Unfortunately, my parents were killed the week before, and I was too shocked and stumped to go through with the wedding. So, against everyone's advice, I insisted on postponing it. Then, as time went on, I kept refusing to set another date. I don't know why — I just couldn't face a wedding without Mom and Dad. Randy argued with me, his mother and father reasoned with me, but to no avail. I just wanted to be left alone, and I wouldn't join Randy in the usual summer activities of the young crowd. I seemed to have lost my capacity for enjoyment of everything. I wasn't even sure I still loved Randy. But I never told him that. However, I can see now that he must have sensed it.

Finally, in August, I sold our home in Hartsdale, where I had been living since my parents' death, cared for by a trusted servant who had been with us for ten years. I found her another job with some friends of my mother and moved into the city in an apartment in the Peter Cooper complex on First Avenue and Twentieth Street. I took the best of the furniture with me, sold some and put the rest in storage against the time when Randy and I would eventually marry.

He had begged me not to move into the city but to marry him and get an apartment for the two of us in White Plains. But something held me back, so he continued to live at home with his family in Scarsdale, and I moved into the city.

I took a course in stenography and typing, and after a while I got a job in an advertising agency. Of course Randy was very much opposed to all this, but I went through with it anyway. In the meantime he had gotten a job with General Foods in White Plains, some sort of managerial position. He had majored in Business Management at Cornell.

I never would admit it, but I was lonely in

the city. I saw Randy only on Sunday when he drove down to take me out to dinner. Through the week he said he was too busy to get away, often working overtime at the office.

Then one Sunday he didn't come down to see me, and I didn't hear from him. I waited all day, not having any dinner because I expected him to arrive at any minute. Finally, about five in the afternoon, I called his home. His mother answered. I knew her well enough to feel free to ask her what, if anything, had happened to Randy. She hesitated, then asked, "Didn't Randy call you?"

I said, "No."

There was another hesitation on her part before she said, "Well, I'd just like to shake him!"

I said, "Oh? Why?"

She sighed. "Well, I suppose I might as well tell you; I know he has dreaded having to. He's been seeing a lot of Lillian Kent, down the road from us, since you moved into the city, and — well, he is going to marry her. It will be announced in next week's papers."

I felt suddenly faint, and my hand holding the receiver began to tremble. I had been wondering if I still loved Randy, and now, all of a sudden, I realized I didn't want to lose him. Which was, of course, selfish of me. I said, "Oh! Well, congratulate him for me."

As I started to drop the receiver into place, I heard Mrs. Winthrop say, "I'm sorry, Judy."

Somehow I managed to get through the evening and the following week, but my job in the advertising agency went suddenly stale on me. Then, to complicate things even more, the account executive whose secretary I was lost his biggest account, and I was going to have to look for another job. I registered with a couple of employment agencies, but they didn't come up with anything. Then a couple of Sundays later I saw an ad in the paper for a secretary to a writer in an upstate village. It said, *Room and board. Secluded, quiet area, beautiful surroundings.*

I answered it and received an answer from a Leslie Terrell, who I took for granted was a woman. And that is how I happened to be there.

But to get back to the present, Leslie said, "We'll go upstairs right after breakfast, and I'll go over for your things later."

I said, "I'd better go with you. I've unpacked some of my things and —"

He said, "All right. I wouldn't know how

to pack women's things."

My time in the lab was very interesting. Leslie's current project was crystals, about which I knew nothing. He explained patiently that crystals, now frequently man-made, are the heart of modern technology.

I knew, of course, that salt and sugar are crystalline. But I didn't know, or hadn't stopped to think, that diamonds and rubies, ice, snowflakes and most minerals and rocks of the earth's crust are also crystalline. Nor did I know that because of their atomic structure, some crystals exert strange forces on light. Nor did I know they possess great strength. Nor did I know that with the aid of crystals, light generates electricity. And on and on.

He showed me how to do an experiment with crystals of ordinary potash alum. I dissolved this chemical in warm water, let it cool and watched it form seed crystals. Then I suspended one tiny seed in a saturated solution. I was to leave it suspended in the solution for two days and then note how the seed crystal had grown.

As I became more and more interested in the subject, I wandered around the lab asking endless questions. Over on a side table was a container of some kind of black stuff. I asked, "What is this?"

He told me, “It’s carbon black. One of its uses nowadays is in tests for cancer. The patient is painted with carbon black; then liquid crystals are daubed on the black. The tests may help outline cancerous areas, which are usually warmer than benign tumors. Temperature differences show up as varying colors. The cool areas appear red, and intermediate temperatures register green. Other parts show up blue.”

I couldn’t help but remember the black on my face after the thunderstorm. I also remembered the ghostly hand I’d seen over by the Buddha that glowed in the dark and radiated colors: green, red and blue.

I backed away from him, and there must have been fright in my eyes, because he asked, “What’s the matter?”

With an effort I got myself under control and turned away. “Can we go over to the other house now and get my things?” I asked.

He said, “Yes, come on.” Wordlessly I followed him out of the lab and down to the car. We said very little as we drove over to the brick house. When we reached there, the front door was wide open, and the entrance hall was buzzing with flies. Leslie said, “I thought you said you were locked out last night.”

"I was." I went into the bedroom to pack my bags hastily, and Leslie went upstairs to take a look around. I finished before he came down, put my bags in the entrance hall and wandered into the living room. I'd have to take the galleys and the stenographer's notebook, and I'd left them on the table-desk last night. But at the door to the living room, my heart seemed to stop beating and I couldn't even scream. Then slowly, deliberately, though reluctantly, I walked over to the body that was lying on the floor before the table on which was the Buddha of Fertility. It was a girl, Gail Ferguson. And there was a switch-blade knife in her heart. Blood had oozed out around the wound, stained the white turtleneck shirt and trickled down onto the floor. The girl's eyes were closed, and on each lid lay an emerald — undoubtedly the emeralds from the eyes of the Buddha.

I heard Leslie run down the stairs, calling, "Miss Carson," but I couldn't speak. When I didn't answer him he strode around the apartment until he found me in the living room, standing staring down at the corpse of his cousin Gail.

He reached me and caught me in his arms just as my knees gave way. I didn't faint; I just sagged, because my legs suddenly lost all their strength. He helped me over to the sofa, sat me down, then returned to the dead body of his cousin. He knelt down and examined the knife but didn't touch it. He started to touch one of the emeralds, then thought better of it. When he got to his feet, I asked, "Are you going to call the police?"

He stood looking down at me thoughtfully, and I wondered what was going through his mind. After a long silence he said, "Not just yet. I don't want them poking around up here." There was a gleam in his eyes that chilled my blood.

I said, "Hadn't you better start the police on a search for Roger?"

He looked at me in complete astonishment. "Whatever for?"

I shrugged. "Well, couldn't *he* have killed her?"

He kept looking at me, and began to shake his head as if he couldn't believe what he had heard. "But he loved her! Why would he kill her?"

"I wouldn't know. But lots of people kill someone they love because of — oh, because of lots of reasons."

One of the emeralds fell off the left eyelid of the corpse and hit the floor with a faint click. It rolled a little, then came to rest in a pool of drying blood.

Leslie turned around and saw it winking as a shaft of sunlight from a window struck it. He started toward it. I said, "Don't touch it. It may have fingerprints on it."

"Oh! Don't be ridiculous! It's too small." But he stopped, stared down at it, then came and sat down on the sofa beside me. He slid down so his head was resting on the back and stretched his long legs out in front of him. His big hands lay limply on the seat beside his thighs. I didn't know what to say or do. Then I saw tears were running down his cheeks, and his firm, nicely shaped lips were tight together to keep them from trembling. I wondered if he had loved the dead girl, in other than a cousinly way. He answered my unspoken question by saying, "If she hadn't been my cousin, I would have married her after we grew up."

I put a hand on his, resting between us on the sofa. "I'm sorry," I said.

He sat up, pulling his hand from beneath mine. "Don't be. It would have been a mistake. We would never have made a go of it."

He stood up, walked over to the dead girl and stood looking down at her. "I suppose I'll have to call the police." He turned and walked over to the desk, stopped, stared out of the window and watched a robin hopping across the lawn. "I wonder where Roger is?"

he said, more to himself than to me.

"Could he be hiding on the property?"

He whirled around angrily. "What do you mean by that?"

I shrugged. "If *she* came back, wouldn't *he* have too?"

He turned to the window again. "The motorcycle isn't anywhere around."

"What about the guitar?"

"That isn't either."

"Do they — I mean — did they both play it?"

"Yes."

"Do they only have one between them?"

"Yes. It's a very special one, made to order for them."

"But they both know how to play it?"

"Oh, yes."

"This building doesn't have a garage, does it?"

"No."

"That brown shingle barn over by your house — could he and the motorcycle and the guitar be there?"

"I keep it locked. No one can get in but myself. I park my car in the front. Besides, there is no reason why Roger should hide. He didn't kill his wife."

"How do you know?"

"Because he isn't a killer."

"Doesn't everyone have the potential, with enough provocation?"

"I don't believe that."

"Could he be dead, too?"

He turned on me then. "Are you crazy?" he demanded. "Who would kill *him?*"

"Perhaps the same person who killed Gail."

He took a step toward me, and for a moment I thought he was going to hit me. Then the belligerence went out of him. "Are you hinting *I* might have killed them both?"

"Of course not. But how well did you know either of them? Do you know their friends? Their enemies?"

He sat on the edge of the desk and rammed his hands in his trouser pockets. "I don't know much about Roger," he said. "Gail met him in Greenwich Village at one of those coffeehouses. He used to entertain there. He told her he came from Brooklyn, that his father had a gas station there somewhere, that his mother was a waitress in a bar and grill."

"And Gail?"

"She had a good home in Westport, Connecticut. I told you. I stayed with them for a while when I first came back from Indo-China. Her mother was my mother's sister. Her father is in Wall Street. He's a statistician."

"Were they — Gail and Roger — on pot or something?"

"He was. As far as I know, she wasn't."

"Would you have known?"

"I think I could have seen the signs."

"Was there any reason for her to leave home?"

"None whatever. Her parents were good to her, worshipped her and each other." He sighed. "But that doesn't seem to be enough for kids these days."

"Aren't you and I of the same generation?"

"No. Not quite. There is just enough difference to make a gap. Sometimes just a year will do it."

"If the police come into this, what will it do to your lab work?"

A frown creased his forehead. "Ruin everything, if I should have to stop work now and go into court and all that."

"That would be too bad."

"It would mean I would have to start all over again on this particular project."

"Shouldn't you notify Gail's parents?"

A look of horror came over his face. "Oh, my God!" he cried. "I never thought of that. Of course."

"Do you want me to call them for you?"

"No. It's my job." He glanced over at the

dead girl and shook his head, chewing at one side of his lower lip.

I asked, "What are you going to do about the emeralds?"

He shrugged. "What *can* I do?"

"I mean — well, they belong to you. And you say they are valuable. Are you going to let the police take them?"

"Why not? They are evidence."

"The kind that might point to you."

He glanced at me. "That's a nice thing to say."

"You have to face facts."

"Do you want out before the police arrive? I can drive you down to the village, even to the hotel in Cobleskill, if you want."

I felt rebuked. "No, of course not. I can't leave you now."

"Why not?"

"Well, I don't want to leave you alone to face this."

An expression came into his eyes that caused my heart to leap. Then, as quickly as it had cone, it was gone, and he said, "*You* will be questioned, you know. We will both be suspect."

"But I wasn't here when it happened."

"Can you prove that?"

"I was with you. You know that."

"I don't know what you did after I left you

in the guest room last night. You could have slipped out and come over here."

"So could you."

"That's right. I could have."

"You could have killed her before you came over here last night."

"Won't the coroner be able to tell how long she has been dead?"

"I suppose so, approximately."

There was silence between us for a few moments; then I asked, "Do you think the emeralds had anything to do with it?"

"Why should they?"

"Well, they were stolen right out of the Buddha's head. Then they suddenly appear on the dead girl's eyes. It's almost as if it were a challenge from the murderer."

He didn't answer me, so I went on, "They must have been taken because someone wanted to sell them to get money, maybe for drugs. Then perhaps the girl — er, Gail — put up an argument about it and got killed because of it. Then the thief, who could also be the murderer, didn't dare try to sell them, so he gave them back." I couldn't help shivering a little at the vivid picture I'd drawn of the crime and the ensuing tragedy.

Leslie looked at me thoughtfully for a moment; then he turned and picked up the black phone, gave the operator a Westport,

Connecticut number and stood waiting for the connection. But before he got it, suddenly the quiet of the room was shattered by the explosive sounds of a motorcycle. Leslie dropped the phone and strode out to the porch, and I after him, just as Roger zoomed to a stop and got off the motorcycle. As soon as he shut off the motor, Leslie demanded, "Where have you been?"

Roger pulled off his helmet and wiped the sweat off his forehead with a not too clean hand. "Down in the city," he said. "I had a job on a late TV special last night. Don't you ever watch TV?"

Leslie said, "Not if I can help it. Haven't you noticed I don't have one up here? Where's Gail?"

Roger shrugged. "I don't know. That's why I came back. Isn't she here?"

Leslie's lips tightened. "Is she supposed to be?"

Roger made an impatient movement. "How should I know?"

"You're her husband. Why wouldn't you know?"

A sullen look came into Roger's eyes. "We had a fight," he said.

"Wasn't she on the show with you?"

"No. That's what we had the fight about. She was mad because they didn't take us as a team. She didn't want me to do a single. It was a rush job. The scheduled singer got sick." He began unbuttoning his black leather jacket, and I saw that around his neck, over a white turtleneck sweater, was the inevitable string of love beads.

Leslie stood looking at him thoughtfully for a moment. Then he asked, "Why did you take the emeralds?"

Roger looked genuinely surprised. "What emeralds?"

"The ones in the eyes of the Buddha."

"Are you nuts or something? I didn't even know they *were* emeralds. I thought they were just glass."

"No, they were emeralds. Oriental emeralds."

Roger turned and parked the motorcycle against the porch steps at the side. I noted the fact that he didn't have the guitar with him. Turning back to Leslie, he asked, "What would I want with emeralds, for heaven's sakes?"

"To sell. To get money."

Roger pushed his long hair away from his face. "I got money," he said. "I don't have to steal to get it. I'm an artist, an entertainer. I get paid good."

"Would Gail have wanted them for anything?"

Roger took a menacing step toward Leslie, and I inadvertently moved closer to him. "Man, are you crazy or something?" Roger yelled at him. "Accusing Gail of stealing your lousy emeralds!" His fists were clenched, and my heart began to pound, but Leslie stood his ground. "No, I am not crazy, and I am not accusing anybody of stealing the emeralds, but I *would* like to know who took them."

Roger relaxed a little. "Well, *I* didn't and Gail didn't." Then he looked at me. "What about *her?* She's new up here, isn't she? And the Buddha is in the apartment she's living in."

This time Leslie took a step toward Roger, and now *his* fists were clenched. "You leave *her* out of it!" he cried angrily.

Frightened now, I put a restraining hand on his arm, and for several moments the two men angrily confronted each other. Then I said quietly to Leslie, "Hadn't you better tell him?"

"Tell me what?" Roger demanded, glancing at me with eyes that looked glassy.

Leslie drew in a short breath. "That Gail came back here."

"She did? Where is she?" Then, without waiting for an answer, he shoved us both aside and rushed up onto the porch and into the house. Leslie and I both rushed after him, trying to catch him, but he pulled angrily away from us and went into the entrance hall and up the stairs to the second floor, two steps at a time.

Leslie pulled his lower lip in between his teeth, and we looked at one another helplessly. We were both relieved that Roger hadn't gone into the downstairs living room. Then Leslie ran up the stairs after Roger, saying to me over his shoulder, "You get out of here! Go over to my place."

I shouted, "No!" after him, but he was already on the second floor.

Chapter Four

Not knowing what to do after Leslie and Roger had gone upstairs, I went into the living room and sank down on the sofa. My knees were trembling and I felt kind of sick all over. Reluctantly I glanced over at the dead girl. She was still there, and the eye from which the emerald had fallen had opened. I started to scream, but covered my mouth with both hands. I wanted to get up and run — run over to the white house as Leslie had told me to. Only that wouldn't be far enough away. I wanted to run down the mountain to the village. I almost felt as if I could run all the way to the city. But no matter how far I ran, that staring dead eye would follow me, and I knew I would never want to look at emeralds again.

I could hear footsteps tramping around upstairs; then the two men came running down the stairs and into the living room. Roger was first, whizzing by me with the speed of a bullet. Suddenly he stopped beside the body of his wife. He looked down at her for a moment; then, bowing his head in his hands, he began to cry. The stifled, heart-rending sounds that came from him gave me cold chills. Leslie stood in the center of the room as if frozen there. Then suddenly Roger stopped crying. He took his hands away from his face, turned, and in one animal-like leap attacked Leslie. The two men went down on the floor with a crash, and before I could do anything about it they were fighting viciously. That is, Roger was fighting viciously. Leslie was fighting defensively. I could see he didn't want to hurt Roger, but neither did he want to be killed, and Roger was going to kill him if he could. To keep out of it, I had to pull my feet up onto the sofa, and a couple of times I was afraid the two men were going to roll over onto the corpse.

The first chance I got, when they were fighting far enough away from me so I could get up, I did so, ran up to the second floor and called the police. The two men didn't even know I had left the room, and when I returned they were still at it. I decided I'd better take a hand myself, or by the time the police arrived it would be too late. I began yelling at them, "Stop it!" But neither of them paid any attention to me. I remembered seeing a bag of golf clubs in the entrance hall closet. I ran out to get one, and when I opened the door something fell out on me. It was Gail's guitar. I caught it before it could hit the floor. It must have been put up on the shelf, and when I opened the door it slid off. I didn't return it to the shelf but stood it in a corner, making sure it would stay put. Then I took a mashie iron from the golf bag and ran back to the living room. Roger had Leslie on the floor and was straddled over him, with his hands around Leslie's throat. Running across the room, I swung the club with all my strength so the head of the club hit Roger on the back of his head. His fingers released Leslie's throat, and he collapsed, falling face down on top of the man I suddenly realized I loved. I dropped the club and pulled Roger's inert body off of Leslie, who was now feeling of his throat and trying to sit up. I reached out my hands to help him, and with an effort he managed to stagger to his feet. He shook his head, felt of it with his hands, felt his jaw that was turning blue, and wiped away some blood from his swollen nose. Finally he looked at me and tried to smile. "Thanks," he said. "He packs a mean wallop."

We both looked down at Roger, who hadn't moved since he'd collapsed. In a hoarse whisper I said, "I hope I haven't killed him."

Leslie bent over Roger, felt of him, placed

a hand over his heart. "He's alive," he said. Then he looked up at me. "But why did you hit him?"

"I had to. I couldn't stand by and let him kill you."

"He wouldn't have."

"He would have, and you know it. You fight too fair. He doesn't." I picked up the golf club, and took it out to the hall closet and replaced it in the bag. When I returned to the living room, Leslie was dialing a number on the black phone. When he got it, he said, "Mary? Leslie Terrell. Is my aunt there? She isn't? Do you know where she is? They were coming up here? Do you know why? You don't? That's too bad. Me? Oh, I'm fine but — well, I'm afraid I have some bad news for them. About Gail. She's — well, she came up here the day before yesterday, but she didn't stay long. Oh, she did? She came over to Westport? When was that? Last evening? When did she leave? Oh! Yes — yes, she came back here. I don't know how to tell you this, but she had an accident. No, it wasn't the motorcycle. Yes, I'm afraid it is serious. How long ago did the folks leave? Oh. Then they should be here any minute. Yes, I'll be here." He dropped the phone into place and stood staring out of the window. A dirty white police car with two revolving lights on the roof drove up the road and stopped in front of the house, and two policemen got out.

Leslie turned to me, his eyes suddenly flashing angrily. "Did you call them?" he demanded.

I murmured, "Yes. I had to. I was afraid Roger would kill you."

At our feet Roger stirred, groaned, rolled over and managed to sit up, feeling the back of his head where a large lump was beginning to show beneath his untidy hair. There was a loud knock on the front door. I said, "I'll go," and did.

When I opened the door, one of the policemen asked, "Having trouble here?"

I said, "Yes. Please come in." I led them into the living room, but Roger was gone. There was only Leslie standing beside the table-desk and the corpse of Gail lying on the floor, with her one eye open and staring at nothing, the other closed by the weight of the emerald.

The policemen immediately saw Gail and went over to her. "Who is she?" one of them asked.

Leslie said, "She's my cousin."

"Who killed her?"

"I don't know."

There was the sound of another car stopping out in front. It parked behind the police car, and a man and woman got out. The man was heavy-set, with thinning brown hair sprinkled with gray. He looked around forty-five. He had on an Hawaiian print shirt and tan slacks. The woman was small, with a nice figure for her age, which was easily over forty. Her hair was a soft honey blonde brushed back from her small-featured face and combed into a roll at the nape of her neck. She was wearing a yellow shirtwaist dress and matching yellow shoes.

One of the policemen, glancing out the window, asked, "Who are they?"

Leslie said, "The girl's parents. Mr. & Mrs. Wakefield. Mrs. Wakefield is my aunt."

"Do they live here?"

"No. They live in Westport, Connecticut."

"Why have they come here?"

"Why shouldn't they? They are relatives of mine. They visit me from time to time." He went to greet them. In a moment he led them into the room. He had an arm around the woman's shoulders. When she saw the body of the girl lying on the floor, she uttered a strangled gasp and, wrenching away from Les, ran across the room and dropped on her knees beside the dead girl. “Oh, my baby!” she wailed, and put out a shaking hand to touch the white face and close the lid of the eye that was open. Then she drew back, got to her feet with the aid of a policeman and began backing away from the corpse. “That isn’t Gail!” she cried.

She turned to her husband, who put his arms around her. “Of course it’s Gail,” he said, looking over her head at the dead girl lying on the floor. Then suddenly he put his wife from him, strode over, hunched down on his heels and examined the corpse carefully. When he got up, he said, “She’s right. That isn’t our daughter Gail.” I caught a quick look of understanding pass between them, but it was gone in a flash.

We all turned to Leslie — his aunt and uncle, the two policemen and I. “Of course it’s Gail!” he said crossly. “Who else would it be?”

His aunt said stubbornly. “It isn’t Gail.”

I couldn’t help saying, “But Roger said it was Gail.”

Leslie gave me a quick glance, saying, “He didn’t actually *say* it was Gail in so many words, but he acted as if it was.”

The policeman asked, “Who is Roger?”

“He is her husband.”

“Where is he?”

Leslie said, "I don't know. He went to the bathroom."

"Where is that?" the policeman asked.

Leslie led him to the bathroom which opened off of my bedroom. In a moment they returned. The policeman said, "There isn't anyone there."

I said, "Maybe he went upstairs."

Leslie shook his head. "You would have seen him if he'd gone into the entrance hall, wouldn't you?"

I said, "Yes. He didn't. But he could have gone out the back door."

After a thorough search of the building, it was decided Roger was not in it.

The policeman said, "Maybe he went over to your house."

I saw Leslie's lips tighten. I knew he didn't want them going over and searching his house, but there was no way he could stop them. He said to me, "Will you stay here with my aunt and uncle?"

I said, "Yes, of course," wishing someone would do something about the corpse of the girl, whoever she was.

After the police and Leslie had gone, Mr. & Mrs. Wakefield and I sat there in an uncomfortable silence. Then Mrs. Wakefield said, "I suppose you are a new secretary?"

I said, "Yes. I got here just a couple of days ago."

She looked at me steadily for a moment, then said, "If you don't mind me giving you some advice — if you're smart, you'll get down off this mountain as quickly as you can."

Her husband said, "Keep still, Margaret."

"No. I won't keep still. She looks like a nice girl, and this is no place for her."

"But why?" I asked. "Mr. Terrell seems to be a very nice man. I like the job, and I like it up here."

"Leslie *is* a nice boy," she said. "But it isn't as nice up here as it looks. He never should have bought this horrible mountain top! It's haunted and it's evil. I can feel it all around me every time I come up here. And I've always been worried every time Gail came up here."

"But why? I don't believe in ghosts, if that's what you mean."

"It's more than just ghosts." She glanced uneasily at the dead girl and shuddered. "Look at her — if you need any more proof."

"But she was murdered."

Mrs. Wakefield nodded. "And it could easily have been my daughter Gail, or you."

Her husband put a hand on hers, which

were clasped tightly in her lap. "There, there," he said gently. "Don't go imagining things."

I was curious about how the Wakefields could be so positive the dead girl was not their daughter when she looked exactly like her. I had seen Gail only a couple of times and then just for a few minutes, but as I remembered her she looked like the dead girl who was lying there on the floor. And she had on the same things Gail had worn yesterday: the slacks and the white cotton turtleneck shirt and the love beads. Finally I had to ask, "How can you tell this girl is not your daughter?"

Husband and wife exchanged another quick look, and Mrs. Wakefield said, "Gail has a small red spot on her right eyelid. This girl hasn't." It was from the right eyelid the emerald had fallen.

"But it could easily be covered with makeup," I pointed out.

"No, it couldn't. She tried that and finally gave up. It always showed through anything she put on it. It was a birthmark."

"Wouldn't Leslie, Mr. Terrell, have known about it?"

"He may never have noticed it. We never spoke of it. We were so used to it we just took it for granted."

Another thought occurred to me. I asked, "Is this girl wearing Gail's clothes?"

Mrs. Wakefield looked over at the body of the girl on the floor. "They look like the same things Gail had on last evening when she came to see us. But it is almost a uniform of young people today."

"Could Gail have given the clothes to her? Or lent them? Or could she have stolen them from Gail?"

"*That* I wouldn't know. I don't even know who the girl is. This girl, I mean."

"Your daughter is an entertainer, I understand."

"Yes. She and Roger are folk singers."

"Does she ever have a stand-in? By that, I mean someone who could substitute for her if she had a performance to do and were suddenly taken ill."

Mrs. Wakefield shook her head. "Not that I ever heard of. If either Gail or Roger couldn't go on, the performance was canceled."

The police must have phoned homicide from the white house, because before Leslie and they returned, the entire homicide crew arrived — coroner, a fingerprint man, a photographer and a doctor in an ambulance, together with several detectives. By the time Leslie and the two policemen came back, the horrible but necessary things had been done, and the corpse had been put on a stretcher and covered with a blanket, ready to be taken out to the ambulance. The emerald that was still keeping the girl's left eyelid closed was put on the table beside the Buddha and left there. No one seemed to be at all interested in it, least of all the police.

After the body had been carried out, I saw the emerald that had fallen to the floor. It had been kicked to one side and left, unnoticed by everybody. I went over and picked it up and put it on the table beside the other one. Leslie watched me but didn't say anything.

I had expected the police would question us extensively, but they didn't. As they left, one of them said to Leslie, "We'll be in touch with you." Then he gave each of us a searching look. "Can any of you identify the dead girl?"

We each shook our head. Leslie said, "If she isn't Gail Ferguson, we don't know who she is — was."

The policeman looked at the Wakefields. "Would you swear in a court of law that the girl isn't your daughter? What was her name — Gail Ferguson?"

Simultaneously they said, "Yes."

"Then *where* is your daughter?"

They shook their heads. "We don't know. We seldom know exactly where she is." Then Mrs. Wakefield said, "Do you know where she is, Leslie?"

He said, "No. If I did, I wouldn't have mistaken the dead girl for her."

The policeman started for the door. Over his shoulder he said, "There will be an inquest. You had all better stick around for that."

"But we can't stay here!" Mrs. Wakefield protested. "We have to go home."

The policeman took a notebook and pen out of a pocket and came back into the room. "Your full name, address and phone number," he said.

Mr. Wakefield said, "We are Mr. & Mrs. James Wakefield of Cherry Lane, Westport, Connecticut." He took a card out of his pocket. "The phone number is on this. Also my business address in the city."

The policeman took the card, read it and put it and his notebook and pen into his pocket. "We'll call you," he said, and strode from the house.

When the Wakefields, Leslie and I were left alone, Mrs. Wakefield said, "Well, *now* I hope you will sell this horrible place and move down among civilized people!"

Leslie chewed at his lower lip. "Please,

Aunt Margaret, let me manage my own life. Whoever killed that girl, whoever she was, must have been one of your so-called civilized people and not from this mountain."

"Nonsense! This place is haunted, and everybody around here knows it!"

Leslie smiled at that. "Aunt Margaret," he said, "ghosts or spirits or whatever they are called don't carry switch-blade knives." Then he added, "I called your house just before you got here to ask you to come up because I thought the girl was Gail, and Mary said Gail had been in Westport last evening."

Mrs. Wakefield nodded. "Yes. She seemed to be quite upset about something, but she wouldn't tell me what it was."

"According to Roger, it was because he had a job on a TV special last evening as a single, and she didn't want him to do it without her."

Mr. Wakefield lit a cigarette. "We saw it. He was very good. He made quite a thing out of not having his guitar and borrowed one from a member of the orchestra."

"Was Gail still here? I mean, did she see the show with you?"

Mrs. Wakefield shook her head. "No. It was a late show. She only stayed about an hour, packed a bag of her clothes that she keeps in her old room, and took off."

"On the motorcycle?"

"No. She had her Volkswagen. Roger won't ride in it. He prefers that horrible motorcycle."

Leslie smiled. "Yes, I know."

Mrs. Wakefield turned to her husband. "Well, we'd better go. We have a long drive."

He said, "Yes, we'd better get started."

Suddenly Leslie asked, "Just why did you come up here?"

Husband and wife exchanged a glance, and then Mrs. Wakefield said, "Well, we were worried about Gail. She acted so strangely last night, and she said she was coming up here. So we just couldn't help coming up to see if we could find out what was wrong. We thought you would know."

Leslie said, "All I know is what I've told you."

Mr. Wakefield said, "Well, we'll see you at the inquest. They will probably have it in a couple of days. But I don't know what we can tell them that will help any."

Just before they got into their car, to which Leslie and I had accompanied them, Mrs. Wakefield said, "If you see or hear from Gail, let us know right away."

Leslie said, "Yes, I will."

He and I stood side by side and watched

their car disappear around a bend in the road. Then Leslie said, “Now I’d better drive you down to the village. You will be able to catch the four o’clock bus to Albany and connect with a New York bus.”

I stared at him, my stomach feeling as if the bottom of it were full of lead. “But I can’t leave now. You heard what the policeman said. We are all supposed to stick around following the inquest.”

His mouth tightened at the corners. “Then I’ll take you over to Cobleskill. You can stay at the hotel. I’ll pay for it. But I can’t let you stay up here after what has happened.”

“But it had nothing to do with me. There would be no reason for anyone to harm me.”

“Then why were you knocked over the head last night? You must have been in somebody’s way.”

“I don’t know. Who is it?”

“If I knew that, I’d probably know who the murderer is.” He sighed. “Well, come on then; we’ll go back to my place. Where are your bags?”

I pointed to them. They were still at the side of the entrance hall where I had put them a few hours ago — a space of time which seemed to have lasted a lifetime.

Chapter Five

When we got back to the white house, Leslie said, "I could use a drink of something stronger than iced tea. How about you?"

I collapsed on the sofa in the living room. "Yes, I could too."

He went to a cabinet in a corner, fixed drinks of Scotch on the rocks and came and sat beside me. I asked, "Did the police bother your lab when they came over here?"

He said, "No. Fortunately they didn't. As we came to the door, I said, 'This is just my lab.' I opened the door, and they glanced around and let it go at that."

"Did they search that old brown shingle barn?"

"Yes, *that* they did search. But there was no one there."

"And no sign of the motorcycle?"

"No."

"Where do you think Gail is?"

"I wouldn't even hazard a guess. She may be in their apartment down in the city — in Greenwich Village."

I bounced on the sofa and slopped some of my drink down the front of me, and

Leslie gave me his handkerchief to wipe it off. "Of course!" I cried. "Why didn't somebody think of that?"

Leslie shrugged. "We haven't had much time to think," he said.

"No, we haven't."

Then I asked a question that surprised him. "Do you know much about your aunt and uncle?"

"That's a strange question."

"Yes, I suppose so. What I mean is, you said you stayed with them for a while after you came over from Indo-China. I was just wondering, did you ever notice anything strange about them?"

He put his drink on the coffee table and turned to give me a look of surprise; one could almost have termed it a look of consternation. "What are you getting at?" he demanded.

"I don't exactly know, but there was something about them that didn't ring true."

"That's ridiculous!"

"I don't think so." Then I asked another question that astounded him, as well as myself, because the idea seemed to pop into my head from nowhere. "Are you sure those two people are Gail's parents?"

He jumped to his feet and began to pace back and forth in front of me, his huge hands rammed into the pockets of his trousers. "Of course they are!" he yelled at me.

But I wasn't going to be intimidated. An inner premonition warned me that there was something sinister with the whole set-up. I asked, "And are you sure that dead girl isn't Gail?"

He stopped his pacing and stood in front of me, staring at me with an almost blind look in his eyes. After a moment he said, "I was sure until Aunt Margaret said she wasn't."

"Did you ever notice a small red spot on Gail's right eyelid?"

"There might have been. To tell the truth, I never noticed. She always has her eyes so wide open, and I've never seen her asleep."

"According to your aunt and uncle, she did have such a mark. While you were over here with the police, I asked your aunt how she could tell that girl wasn't her daughter, and she said because Gail had a small red spot on her right eyelid and the dead girl didn't. And her husband corroborated her statement."

Les shrugged. "Could be. It must be very small." He stared at me stupidly for a moment; then he turned and started to stride out of the room. I asked, "Where are you going?"

Over his shoulder he said, "To the morgue. You stay here!" But I jumped up and ran after him. "Not on your life!" I cried. "I'm not going to stay here all alone. I'm coming with you!"

Surprisingly enough, he didn't argue with me. In the car, as it bounced over the fields, I asked, "Was the girl who arrived with Roger and later came over here and put oleander leaves in the iced tea Gail Ferguson, or the girl who got murdered, who wasn't Gail?"

Leslie swung the car onto the dirt road. "I don't know. I don't understand how two people can look so much alike — if there are two."

"They say everyone has a double somewhere."

"That's ridiculous!"

"I suppose so."

That was the end of our conversation until we got to the main road; then I asked, "If you decide that girl is really Gail, what are you going to do?"

"I don't know. But if she is Gail, she deserves a decent burial."

"But if her own mother and father refuse to accept her as their daughter — ?"

"Then I'll take care of things myself. After all, whoever she is, she was killed, murdered, in my house."

"If she isn't Gail, the only way to prove it would be to find the real Gail."

"Yes."

"And if she is — there is still Roger to be found."

"That's right."

"Did Gail have any money? I mean, any money besides what she and Roger made from their singing?"

"Not as far as I know."

"She didn't have any inheritance that perhaps someone might get if she died?"

"No."

"But you really didn't know any of them very well. And if you'll pardon me saying so, the Wakefields got you out of the house as quickly as they could and shunted you off to a school."

"Miss Carson," Leslie said sternly, his knuckles whitening as he gripped the steering wheel, "will you please be good enough to mind your own business?" His voice was tight, and, glancing at his face, I saw every muscle in it was also tight.

I subsided beside him. "Sorry," I said meekly. But I didn't feel meek. I felt angry, belligerent to the nth degree. Someone was trying to put something over on this man who was my boss, implicating him in a murder. For as surely as I was sitting in the car beside him, I knew that sooner or later the police would get around to accusing him of that girl's murder. At least it looked that way to me.

The morgue was in the police station. Leslie wouldn't allow me to go in with him, but ordered me sternly to stay in the car.

He was gone only a short time, and when he returned he looked even grimmer than he had when he went in. He got into the car, switched on the motor, and the car zoomed off at a frightening speed. He didn't say a word, and I knew better than to ask any questions.

All the way back to his house on the mountain, we rode in silence. And this time he took to the dirt road, instead of veering off through the fields. He stopped the car in front of the house, ignoring me as if I weren't there. So I got out and followed him, thinking to myself, "Well, at least I'm all packed. If he wants to fire me, let him."

By the time I got into the house, he was talking on the telephone. I stood for a moment in the kitchen. Should I go into the living room, or should I go upstairs to the room I had slept in last night? If I stayed there in the kitchen, I couldn't help but hear what he said on the phone.

I decided to go outside again. I could stroll around and pretend to be looking at the flowers. Of course if I stayed near the house I might still be able to hear him talking on the phone, unless he kept his voice low because of the open windows. So I strolled around the side and in the direction of the old two-story brown-shingled barn.

That was where I made my mistake. I was halfway between the barn and the house when something whizzed past the left side of my head and hit the archery target on the barn door. Instinctively I ducked, but it was too late. The arrow, for that is what it was, was deeply imbedded in the target on the barn door. If it had hit my head, I dared not think what it would have done to me. Perhaps it had been an accident. But no, whoever had shot the arrow from its bow had meant me to be the target. Of that I was certain.

I turned and looked back at the house, from which direction the arrow had seemed to come, but there was no one in sight. Who then, could have shot it? Surely not Leslie Terrell. What object would he have for trying to kill me or even to frighten me? All he had to do to get rid of me would be to fire me, and I would have to go. And if the arrow hadn't been shot by Leslie, then who else was in the house, or near it? And what did he or she have against me? Obviously I was in somebody's way; or I had inadvertently learned too much during my short residence on the mountain. Either that, or somebody was hiding something up there that he or she did not want me to find out about.

I decided I would return to the house. If Leslie was still phoning, that was too bad. I wasn't going to stay outside any longer and be a target for whoever wanted to get rid of me.

As I entered the house, I listened for the sound of Leslie's voice talking on the phone, but the house was quiet. Should I go into the living room? I started, going through the short hallway from which the small bathroom opened. Then I heard the buzzing sound a phone makes when the connection has been severed. I started to run, then stopped at the doorway to the living room. Leslie Terrell was crumpled over the desk, and the receiver of the phone was hanging over the edge, swinging on its twisting wire, as if it had just fallen from Leslie's limp hand. I ran over to him, afraid of what I would find out when I touched him.

He was completely unconscious, but I couldn't discover any reason for it. He didn't seem to have been shot. I dragged a heavy wing chair to the desk and managed to half slide, half lift him into it so I could see the front of him. There was no bullet hole, no knife wound. I opened his shirt to see. And there was no sign of a struggle in the room. From his position when I found him, he must have been struck down from behind while he was phoning. The phone was still making the disconnect buzzing sound, and I put the receiver back on the cradle. I wondered if he had gotten his number. When I'd gone out, he had been asking the operator for it. I knew the phone company wouldn't trace the call for me, but perhaps later the police could have it traced.

Leslie's head was hanging down; his chin was on his chest. Gently I lifted it up and rested it in the corner of the wing and the back of the chair. I put my hand inside his opened shirt over his heart. It was beating slowly. I went to the liquor cabinet, found a bottle of brandy, poured some into a small glass and went and held it to his lips, attempting to get some of it into his mouth. I did get a little between his lips, but I got more down the front of him. It must have been the cold of the liquid running down his bare chest that he felt rather than the few drops that had gone between his teeth, because he slowly opened his eyes, groaned, then pushed me away.

I asked, "Are you all right?"

He drew in a long breath, sat up, felt of the back of his head with his left hand, and said, "Ouch!" Then, looking up at me, he asked, "What did you do that for?"

"Spill the brandy on you?"

He touched his lips with his tongue. "No — hit me over the head."

"I didn't. Did you shoot an arrow at me?"

He shook his head, looking puzzled. Then, putting his head against the back of the chair, he closed his eyes. "Didn't shoot an arrow. Don't play games."

"It was no game. Somebody shot an arrow at my head while I was outside. Luckily, it missed me and hit that archery target on the barn door."

He opened his eyes again, and this time they were more lucid than before. "What were you doing out by the barn?" he asked.

"Just taking a walk, to get out of the house so you could phone without me listening."

He smiled a little at that. "Nothing you couldn't hear," he said.

"Did you get your party before you were hit?"

"No. There wasn't any answer."

"Would I be prying if I asked whom you were calling?"

"I was calling the Fergusons' apartment in the city. They live on West Eleventh Street between Fifth and Sixth Avenues."

"Did you get anybody?"

"No."

For a moment we just looked at each other; then I asked, "What is out in that barn?"

"Nothing. Tools, old furniture, old tires — stuff like that. Some bales of hay."

"You mean that's what's in sight. What is hidden?"

He stared at me. "What do you mean — what's hidden?"

"I mean, couldn't there be something hidden somewhere, maybe under floor boards, in the walls, up in the hayloft or somewhere? Maybe something that you don't know about?"

"How silly can you get? Why wouldn't I know about anything hidden there?"

"Maybe it was hidden there before you bought the place?"

"But no one has lived up here for years."

"That would make it perfect for a hide-away, wouldn't it?"

He stared at me. "Yes, I suppose it would. But what could be stashed away there that I wouldn't have discovered?"

"I don't know. How long have you owned the place?"

"A little over a year."

"And has anything unusual happened up here since you've lived here?"

"No. Not until —" he gave me a searching and somewhat surprised look, then added "— not until you arrived."

"Something must have happened over at the brick house to make my predecessor not want to stay there."

He shrugged. "Oh, just things that go bump in the night. Only her imagination."

"I wonder?" I went closer to him. "Can I look at your head? Did someone hit you? You were unconscious when I found you sprawled over the top of the desk."

"Is that right?" He felt of his head again, and I went close to him and looked at it. There was a swelling, and fingering through his thick hair, I could see a scalp wound. But it wasn't very deep. I said, "I'll get some ice for it," and went out to the kitchen, took some ice cubes and wrapped them in a towel. When I returned, he was standing at a side window looking toward the barn. I went and looked over his shoulder. Then I gave a little gasp. "The arrow is gone!" My voice quavered. "The target is still there, but the arrow is gone."

"If there ever was an arrow."

"I can assure you there was. And it just barely missed my head."

He turned and looked down at me. "Then it must have fallen on the ground. Probably hadn't been shot with enough force to imbed it deeply into the target."

"I'd like to go out and see if I can find it." I turned to go, but he caught hold of my arm. "No! Don't go out again. Stay here with me." Seeing the towel with the ice cubes I was holding in my hands, he said, "I'll sit down so you can put that on my head. Maybe it will stop the aching." He went over to the wing chair and sat down, leaning his elbows on his knees so I could lay the improvised ice bag on the back of his head. But it wouldn't stay in place, so I stood and held it for a few minutes, then sat on the arm of the chair. "Does that help any?" I asked.

"A little, maybe because it is freezing the ache."

I wanted to put an arm across his shoulders but dared not. I didn't want to be too familiar. For a while we just sat there; I was holding the now thoroughly soaked towel as the ice cubes melted from the warmth of my hand and his head. After a while I asked,

"Don't you have a plastic bag — a sandwich bag or something like that? If the ice cubes could be put into something leakproof, the towel wouldn't get so wet."

"There might be something like that in the pantry. But I guess that's enough for now, anyway. And thank you."

"It isn't anywhere near enough," I protested. "If you were in the hospital, they would leave an ice bag on your head all night." Come to think of it, my own head didn't feel too good from the bang I'd had the night before. But I couldn't worry about that now.

Leslie pushed me away and stood up. "Well, I'm not in the hospital," he said somewhat crossly.

I had to let him go and was left with the soaking wet towel in my hands. I took it out to the kitchen and threw it in the sink. Then I opened a couple of drawers to find a dry towel. I didn't find the towels, but I did find a pistol. I quickly closed the drawer. I suppose anyone all alone in such an isolated location would be apt to have a weapon of some sort handy.

It was after we'd had supper and were sitting out on the side porch that I saw a light in the barn. The sun had set, and it was almost dark. For a few moments I watched the light, thinking it might be a reflection from the sun. But the sun had long since disappeared behind the peak of the distant mountain and was too far gone to be able to cast such a bright reflection.

When I said, "Can you see that light in the barn?" Leslie replied, "Yes, I've been watching it. Somebody is up in the hayloft."

"What are you going to do about it?"

"Nothing."

"Then you know who is in there?"

"No, of course not."

"And you are sure the barn is always locked?"

"Yes."

I began to get angry. "Are you putting me on?" I asked.

"Not at all."

"Well, something queer is going on up here on this mountain, and it seems to me you are taking it all very casually. Either you know something you aren't telling, or you're too chicken to investigate and find out!"

He gave me a long thoughtful look before saying, "You know, I could fire you for that."

I met his eyes unflinchingly. "That's right, you could. And I'd have to go — that is, until the police subpoenaed me to come back and testify at the inquest."

His eyes narrowed, and he looked almost sinister. "If you've discovered something you are not telling me or the police, you'd better spill it before you end up like that other girl."

"Then you've decided she isn't Gail?"

He gave me a quick look. "What makes you say that?"

"Because when you came out of the morgue you didn't say anything, one way or the other. Now you speak of her as 'that other girl.' If it was Gail, you'd say, 'like Gail.' "

He suppressed a smile. "Think you're real smart, don't you?"

"I'm not exactly dumb. What made you decide?"

"I gave her a ring when we were in high school. She wore it until recently on her right pinky. But as she grew up, her fingers became larger and she couldn't get it over the knuckle. Recently she had it filed off, and you could still see the indentation where the too small ring had made a dent in the flesh."

"Wouldn't her mother have known that?"

"I doubt if she ever noticed Gail was no longer wearing the ring. She isn't the most observing person in the world."

"Well, if you ask me, I think it is all very peculiar."

"No one is asking you. But just watch your step."

"Are you threatening me?"

"No. Just warning you."

"That you are the villain or the murderer?"

"Is that what you think?"

Suddenly I was crying, at first silently, then audibly, sobbing with all the pent-up emotion that had been accumulating for the last forty-eight hours, since I'd first arrived on the mountain top

My employer offered me no sympathy. He just sat there and watched the light in the barn, which seemed to be moving around from time to time, as if it were being pointed in different directions.

At last I stopped crying. I dried my eyes on a piece of Kleenex I had in a pocket and blew my nose. Then I jumped up. "I don't care whether you like it or not, but *I* am going out to that barn and find out who is there. Will you please give me the key?"

He grabbed my arm. "Don't be a fool!" he cried. "Hasn't enough damage been done without you trying to get yourself killed?"

"Then you think someone is out there?"

"Lights don't go on and off by themselves."

"You know who it is?"

He hesitated. "I have my suspicions."

"But you're not going to do anything about it?"

"No."

"Why?"

"Because if it is who I think it is, I don't want to catch them."

I stared at him unbelievingly. "Do you think whoever is out there killed that girl?"

"No. That was something else." Our eyes met and held. Finally I asked, "Why won't you level with me?"

"Because I can't. Not yet. If you'll only trust me, it will be all over in a few days."

"After the inquest?"

"Maybe before."

Suddenly I felt deflated, empty, limp. I said, "Is it all right if I go up to my room? I'm very tired. I'd like to go to bed."

He said, "Yes, but lock your door, and no matter what happens during the night, don't come out."

I was walking toward the door into the hall when I turned back. "Then you do expect something to happen?"

"Not necessarily. But at this point nothing would surprise me. And — well, I don't want anything to happen to you." Then he stood up. "I'll bring your bags."

I had laid the galley proofs and the stenographic notebook on a table, and I picked them up. He followed with my bags. When we were on the second floor, he said, "If you want to use the bathroom or take a shower before you go to bed, I'll wait for you in the lab." I threw him a surprised look. "I want to be sure you are safe in your room before I go downstairs."

I said, "All right. And thanks." I put the galleys and the notebook on the bed in my room, got my toothbrush and things from the smaller of my bags which he had put on the luggage stand, and went along to the bathroom. When I came out he was walking along the hall from the lab. "All set?" he asked.

I said, "Yes. I'll be okay now until morning." I went into my room, turning at the door, and for a moment we stood looking into each other's eyes. Then he took my face between his two hands and gently kissed my lips. At his touch I drew in my breath, then held it until he released me. "You're a sweet girl," he said gently. "Now go to bed. I'll wait here until I hear you lock the door."

I turned away, closed the door and locked it. From the outside he called, "Good night."

"Good night." I stood looking around the room. It was still early, and I wasn't sleepy, even though I was tired, so I went and sat in a chair by one of the windows, turned on the lamp on a nearby table and began to read a couple of the galleys. Then I began leafing through the stenographer's notebook. My predecessor used the same shorthand I did, and I could read most of her notes. They consisted of letters about plastics and later about crystals. One of them was to Miss Gail Ferguson at a West Eleventh Street address in the city. It read:

"Dear Gail:

"If you think those little lumps on your hand and face are cancerous, you should by all means go to your doctor for tests. If you would like me to try the carbon black and liquid crystal test on you first, I will be glad to, but only if you will promise to go to your doctor in New York if my tests show active areas. After all, I am not a doctor.

"Come up any time. And I think you should tell your folks and Roger. That isn't anything to fool around with. However, I think it is all in your imagination. What you really need is a psychiatrist."

I felt tears come to my eyes. So that was it. Gail, the beautiful, talented Gail Ferguson, thought she had cancer. But Leslie could have told me that. If he had dictated that letter to my predecessor, why couldn't he tell me? Then it must have been Gail over at the brick house whose skeletal hand I'd seen near the Buddha and whose cold, carbon black-painted hand touched my face. Les must have known that or suspected it. Why hadn't he told me? And why would she have had that stuff on her over at the brick house? The logical place for the experiment would be in the lab over here.

I leafed through a few more pages of the notebook until my eyes were stopped by a personal note my predecessor had written to a friend of hers. She must have been in the habit of thinking in shorthand, then typing it out, even when she was writing a personal letter. This one said:

"Dear Fanny:

"Don't be surprised if I return home unexpectedly. This is a queer place, and strange things go on. The house I am living in is supposed to be haunted by an Indian girl named Singing Bird who died at least one hundred and fifty years ago, but I have my doubts. I wouldn't be particularly afraid of a ghost, not if it was a friendly ghost. But a ghost who deliberately tries to frighten me by pulling my hair at night when I am sleeping and who puts spiders in my bedroom slippers and who steals my food while I am over at the other house — that kind of a ghost is too human for me. And there is something about a chest of drawers that came from Indo-China. One morning when I got up, the doors to it were open, and one of the drawers was upside down on the floor. That was how I discovered it had a false bottom. But when I told Mr. Terrell, he said I was just imagining it all. I must have had a nightmare. I tell you I don't like it."

I slammed the notebook shut. "Of course!" I said aloud. "Why didn't I think of that? Why didn't Leslie? Or maybe he knew and was just keeping it to himself. If anyone wanted to hide something — drugs, jewels, almost anything small — what better place than the Oriental chest of drawers?

I wondered if I could get out of the house after Leslie went to bed and walk over to the brick house. I would like to do a little bit of investigating myself. But on second thought, I realized that would be a foolish thing to do. If I got myself killed over there, it wouldn't help anybody or solve any of the problems we were facing. I would sleep on it, and in the morning I would suggest the possibility of the chest being a hide-away for something — something valuable and without a doubt unlawful.

Chapter Six

In the morning I waited for Les to call me for breakfast, but he didn't. And I hadn't heard him moving around in the bathroom. So I went downstairs. He was nowhere in sight. Perhaps he was up in the lab. I'd just have to wait. In the meantime I fixed myself some breakfast. There wasn't any sign that he had had any. I made enough coffee for two and mixed a fresh pitcher of concentrated frozen orange juice.

As I looked out of a window toward the barn, everything seemed quiet and normal. After I finished breakfast, I decided to walk out there and look for the arrow that had been shot at me. It wasn't anywhere around. I peeked in a window. There was nothing to see but the inside of an empty barn with a raftered ceiling, a splintered old wooden floor of wide boards and a few bales of hay. Leslie's car was gone. Strange I hadn't heard him go. Or had he gone in the middle of the night while I was asleep? Perhaps he had driven over to the brick house. I decided I'd walk over. I wanted to tell him about the Oriental chest of drawers. If he wasn't there, I would do a little investigating on my own.

It was a beautiful morning. Bright blue sky, not a cloud anywhere, and the air was so clear you could see for miles — surely into the next county.

As I walked over the fields, the grass was still dew-wet, not yet dried by the sun that would later beat down on the mountain top with a burning heat.

When I was near the brick house and could see the front of it, I discovered Leslie's car was not there. Then it dawned on me that if he wasn't there, I wouldn't be able to get in. I didn't have a key. How stupid could I be? But I kept on going. Something unexplainable seemed to be pulling me.

By the time I reached the house, I was tired. The sun had warmed even as I had been walking over the fields. And to my surprise, I saw the front door of the house was ajar. Perhaps Leslie *was* there. He could have walked over. But if he had, where was his car?

I heard the singing and the guitar as I came up the porch steps. Then I began to run. The sounds were coming from my living room. I stopped at the door. There on the sofa sat Gail Ferguson, cross-legged, singing in a low throaty voice and twanging on her guitar. "Where have you been?" I demanded.

She stopped singing, but her fingers continued to twang the guitar strings. "What business is it of yours?" she asked with a toss of her head that sent her long, straight blonde hair back across her shoulders. Her greenish-blue eyes challenged me defiantly. She was wearing the same clothes she'd had on the last time I had seen her; the black pants, white cotton knit turtleneck shirt and the love beads — the same as the dead girl had worn.

I went over and sat down on the sofa beside her. She was turned so she faced me. Without answering her question, I said, "Close your right eye."

"What for?" Her fingers played a few minor chords on the guitar.

"I want to see something."

She closed her right eye, and I saw a small red mark on the lid so high up that unless you were looking for it you might not notice it. "You are Gail Ferguson," I said with a sigh of relief.

"Who did you think I was — Bobbie Gentry?"

"No. But do you know a girl who looks exactly like you, except she hasn't that red spot on her right eyelid?"

Her hands became quiet, and she stared at me. "Why do you ask that, and what gives about the red spot on my eyelid? How do you know about it?"

"Your mother told me."

Gail untwined her legs, put her feet on the floor and placed the guitar in a corner of the sofa. "Where did you see my mother?" She turned back so she was facing me again.

"Here."

"What was she doing here?"

"She came over to see if you were here. Your father was with her."

"Whatever for? I was home only the day before yesterday."

Could she be as innocent as she was pretending? Was she the girl who had put the crushed oleander leaves in the iced tea over at Leslie's? Or was it the girl who had been killed? "You didn't answer my question about a girl who is your double. So you know her?"

She hesitated. Then reluctantly she said, "Yes, I know her. How do *you* know about her?"

"She was murdered here in this room yesterday."

Gail's mouth opened to say something, then closed. She stared at me, her face going as deathly pale as the dead girl's had been. "What did you say?" she asked. Her voice was ragged, as if she couldn't believe what her ears had heard.

"I said, yesterday morning I found a girl who we all thought was you, lying on the floor over there in front of the Buddha of Fertility, with a switch-blade knife in her heart. And on each closed eyelid was an emerald — from the eyes of the Buddha."

For a moment she stared at me; then she got up, rushed out of the room and upstairs. I could hear her upstairs; then she came down slowly and stood in the doorway for a moment. There were tears streaming down her face. "She's gone!" she said.

I said, "Come and sit down. I'll get you a drink."

She came and dropped down on the sofa beside me and put her head back, the way Les had when he'd thought the murdered girl was she.

I got up, went to the liquor cabinet, brought her a drink of brandy and held it to her colorless lips. But she shook her head and pushed my hand away. After a few minutes I asked again, "Who was she?"

She closed her eyes, and the tears kept seeping from beneath the long, darkened lashes. "She was my twin sister," she said.

"But she was mentally deficient, and they had to put her in an institution when she was seven. From then on she was never spoken of at home, and I grew up as if I were an only child."

"How did she get here?"

"I brought her. Since I have been on my own, away from home, I have visited her at least once a month, and recently the doctors said she was improved as a result of some new drugs they had been giving her, and they thought it would be good for her to go home for a while, as an experiment. But Mom and Dad wouldn't have her. They don't want their friends in Westport to know about her. You see, they didn't move to Westport until Carol and I were ten, and by then Carol had been in the institution for three years. Before that we lived in Yonkers."

"Then your mother and father must have known who it was yesterday when they saw her lying dead here on the floor?"

Gail nodded. "I don't see why they wouldn't."

"Perhaps they didn't want to claim her as *theirs*, due to the fact that she had been murdered, and a murder is always given publicity."

Again Gail nodded, and tears kept running down her cheeks. I asked, "You loved her?"

She nodded. "I always thought that there, but by the grace of God, go I. And she was always so sweet. When we were little we were very close. That's the reason they put her in the institution, because they were afraid having us grow up together would affect me and my future life."

"When did you bring her here?"

"The day before Roger and I arrived. I have a car."

"Then she was here in the house when I came? She was here those first two nights I was here, when I thought I was alone?"

Gail nodded. "And so was I."

I shuddered involuntarily, remembering the strange things that had gone on those first two nights. I asked, "Was she in the upstairs apartment?"

"No. You see, I have a key to this house, and there are a couple of old beds up in the attic. I stayed up there with her. And I gave her sleeping pills, so she slept a lot when I wasn't with her."

"Were you here the night of the storm?"

"Yes."

"Was it you who hit me over the head when I went upstairs?"

"No. That was a friend of mine."

"A friend of yours? Who?"

She smiled slyly. "None of your business."

"A man?"

"Wouldn't you like to know?"

"Yes, I would, because somebody carried me downstairs while I was unconscious and left me out on the wet grass and locked me out. And I know you couldn't have carried me alone."

She giggled and tossed back her long blonde hair, and I knew it was useless to try to get the truth out of her. It was almost as if she were a split personality. One minute she was down to earth and sensible; the next she was flighty and impossible.

I asked, "If you were here the night of the storm, when did you leave?"

"About three in the morning. I had my car parked down in the woods."

"Was Carol all right when you left?"

"Yes. I gave her some sleeping pills before I left."

"Was she dressed like you?"

"Yes. She liked wearing my clothes."

"When you left, was your gentleman friend still here?"

"No. He left when I did."

"Did you lock up the house when you left?"

"No, I didn't bother."

"Could your boy friend have come back after you'd gone?"

Her eyes opened wide. "Oh, no! He wouldn't have." Then a cagey look came into her eyes, and under her breath she said, "Oh, no!"

I changed the subject by asking, "Does Leslie Terrell know about your sister?"

"No. We didn't want him to know."

"I see. So even though he didn't know about Carol, you harbored her here on his property, in one of his houses."

"I didn't think he'd mind."

"I'm sure he wouldn't have. But his parents must have known about her."

"They might not have. You see, my mother and my aunt hadn't been friendly after my aunt went to Indo-China, and they never communicated with each other."

"Then how come Leslie was sent to Westport?"

She shrugged. "Just one of those things. I suppose the Heaths had heard that there were some relatives over here, and wrote to Mom and asked her if she'd take Les."

"Does Roger, your husband, know about Carol?"

"No, I never told him."

"Then if he saw her lying dead here on the

floor wearing your clothes, he would think she was you."

She gave me a surprised look. "Did he?"

"Apparently. He cried when he saw her and then he jumped on Leslie and tried to beat him up because he thought Leslie had killed you."

Her face brightened; she stopped crying and smiled. "Did he, really? Did he really care that much?"

"Does that please you?"

She came and sat beside me, still smiling. "Of course. He's been poisonous to me lately, and I never would have dreamed he'd care if I died."

"Do you have any idea why Carol was murdered?"

"None whatever, unless —" a look of fright wiped the smile from her face — "unless somebody thought she was me."

"I thought of that. But who?"

Her face paled. "I don't think Roger would murder me," she said. "We've been fighting a lot lately, but not that badly."

"Do you have any enemies?"

"Not that I know of. I'm not the most popular girl in show business, but I don't think anyone dislikes me enough to murder me."

"If your parents had found out you'd

taken Carol from the institution and brought her here, would they have?"

Her eyes opened wide in horror. "Oh, no! They never would do a thing like that. They loved her, only — well, they were ashamed of having a mentally deficient child."

"But they must realize that if they don't claim her body for a decent burial, she will be buried as — well, whatever they do with people when nobody claims them."

She stared at me for a moment, and I could almost see the wheels clicking around in her head. Finally she said, "I'll claim her. I'll see that she has a decent funeral and is buried in our family plot over near Westport."

"But what about your career in show business? Wouldn't the publicity affect that?"

"No. Besides, I don't care. Carol is more important to me than any old career."

For the first time I felt a slight liking for her. I said, "Leslie said he would see that she had a decent burial, even though he didn't know who she was. He feels responsible because she was killed in his house."

Gail's expression softened. "He *would.* That's exactly like him. He's a —" she sighed "— he's a wonderful guy." She gave me an inquiring look. "Don't you think so?"

I felt a blush warming my cheeks. "He

seems very nice," I said.

"Where is he now?" she asked.

"I don't know. When I got up this morning he was gone. Maybe he went down to the morgue."

"Is that where she is?"

"Yes. At least she was there last evening."

Gail jumped up. "I'd better go down. Where is it?"

"In the police station. On a side street near the main street. I don't know the names of the streets. Probably anyone in the village could tell you. But how will you get there? How did you get up here? The motorcycle isn't around anywhere."

"I have my car, a Volkswagen. I left it down the road a way, in the woods, and walked up. I didn't want anybody to know I was here. I thought you were over at the white house."

"I was."

Then she said a surprising thing. "I'm glad you're here."

"Do you want me to go down to the morgue with you?"

A look of horror crossed her face. "Will I have to see her?"

"No. I don't believe so. Leslie went down last evening."

"But he couldn't have identified her, because he didn't know she even existed."

"No. That's right. But he was going to take care of her burial and everything, even if he didn't know who she was."

Gail chewed at her lower lip for a moment before saying, "So I guess it's up to me to go and identify her. But you don't have to come."

"Perhaps you'd better call your parents and have them come over."

Her eyes hardened. "No! They should have acknowledged her when they saw her here. If they are that ashamed of her, then I don't want any part of them ever again!"

I said, "Oh, you don't mean that. Anyway, you'd better call them and tell them you are all right. They asked Les to call them if he heard from you. Naturally, we were all worried."

"I'll bet. And come to think of it, the only reason Roger got upset when he thought I was dead was because I'm part of his meal ticket."

I couldn't resist saying, "I understand he did a single the other night and went over all right."

She shrugged. "That was just for one time. He couldn't keep it up. He never got anywhere until we were a team. And he knows it."

I had been sitting looking at the Oriental chest of drawers as we talked, and decided that as soon as Gail left to go down to the morgue, I would investigate it.

She said, "Well, I'd better go. When Les comes back from wherever he is, tell him I'm here and that I'll take care of Carol."

"He will want to call your mother."

"Well, let him. But she needn't come running up here to shed crocodile tears over me."

"You know there is going to be an inquest."

She turned at the door. "Oh!" Then she sighed, and her slim shoulders dropped. "Well, I suppose that's inevitable."

"I'm afraid so.

"And there will be an investigation to try to find the murderer."

Her lips tightened, and I could see she was gritting her teeth. "And I'll help with that! Oh, *how* I'll help with that. Why anyone would want to kill poor Carol —" Her voice trailed off. Then she drew in a sharp breath. "Or me," she added.

I said, "Yes. We mustn't forget that. And you'd better be careful. Perhaps you'd better wait for Les to come back and have him go down to the morgue with you."

She thought that over for a moment, then

came back and sat down on the sofa near me. "Maybe you're right. I could be a sitting duck, driving through those woods in my car." She smiled faintly. "It doesn't have bullet-proof windows."

"Somebody tried to kill me with an arrow yesterday," I told her.

She whirled around and stared at me. "With an arrow?" she cried. "How quaint."

"Also lethal, if it had hit my head instead of the target on the barn door."

She laughed. "You're kidding."

"I can assure you I'm not."

"But who would want to kill *you?*"

"I wouldn't know. I thought maybe you might."

"Me? But why *should* I?"

"Because you're in love with Les and jealous of any girl he gets too close to."

She bounced on the sofa, and I was jiggled so my teeth clicked. "You're imagining things," she said crossly. "I have a perfectly good husband. Why should I want Les? Besides, he's my cousin."

"So I've heard."

She leaned over and patted my hands that were clasped in my lap. "Darling," she said, "he's all yours."

I said, "Thanks. And since we're getting so chummy, why did you put crushed oleander leaves in the pitcher of iced tea over at the white house the other afternoon?"

She shrugged. "I wanted to make you sick. I thought if you got sick you'd go away."

"But you could have killed me and Les. Don't you know oleander is poisonous?"

"Sure. But not such a little bit."

"Maybe not. But anything poisonous isn't to be played with."

"Oh, for heaven's sakes!" she said impatiently. "Can't you take a joke?"

"Not that kind." I gave up. There wasn't any use trying to reason with her. So to change the subject, I asked, "Did you ever meet the woman who had my job before me?"

"A couple of times. She was a very negative person. I think Les was glad to get rid of her."

"And what do you know about that Buddha?"

She gave me a startled look. "Nothing much; only that it is supposed to be the Buddha of Fertility and have powers to help barren women bear children."

"That much I know."

For the first time I noticed a slight swelling on the back of her right hand. Was that the place she had thought was cancerous? I asked, "Where have you been between the time you left Westport the other night and now?"

A frown creased her smooth brow. "I don't consider that any of your business."

"I don't suppose it is. But if Les asks you the same question, will you answer him?"

"Yes, I will, because in a way it *is* his business."

I let it go at that and asked, "Did you ever meet the Heaths, the missionaries who took care of Les after his parents were massacred in Indo-China?"

"A couple of times. They stayed up here on the mountain this spring for a while."

"What were they like?"

She shrugged. "Rather nondescript. Tall, thin, gracious, earnest — oh, kind of all sweetness and light. You know. They were all right, but their son Joshua was a creep. He got himself mixed up in local politics wherever they were stationed and had to get out. Something about forming a home guard of the natives and supplying them with guns."

"Did Les ever talk about his life in Indo-China?"

"No. He seemed to want to forget it."

"But he wrote a book about it."

"Yes. But that was to get it out of his system."

"Did you read it?"

"Yes. It was interesting. But it didn't make you want to be a missionary or go to live in Indo-China. Why, do you know they make pets of pigs over there, the way we do dogs? They actually have them in the house."

"No. I didn't know."

"Where are the Heaths now?"

"I haven't the foggiest. Say, what is this anyway — an inquisition, a third degree, or just a questions and answers game?"

"I can assure you it is not a game."

"Then why don't you just mind your own business?" She jumped up from the sofa. "On second thought, I *will* go down to the morgue." She stalked over to the living room door, through the small entrance hall, and in another moment I heard the front door slam. I could see her hurrying down the road in the direction of the woods, her long straight blonde hair streaming behind her.

Chapter Seven

As soon as Gail was out of sight, I went to work on the cabinet. I opened drawer after drawer, finding nothing. Then, quite unexpectedly, my finger touched a spot in one of the drawers with a lid, and the bottom popped up, disclosing several small packages. Each was full of a white powder, and they didn't have to be labeled for me to know what the stuff was. Heroin, of course. But who had hidden it in the cabinet? Did Leslie know it was there? If Roger was an addict, was this the secret hiding place for his supply? And was that why I wasn't wanted here — because I was in the way when he wanted access to it?

What should I do? Leave it in the drawer and pretend I didn't know it was there?

Before I could decide, a man's voice from the doorway to the living room said, "Don't move! I've got you covered."

But I couldn't help looking around. In the doorway and coming slowly toward me was a tall thin man about Leslie's age, wearing a baggy tan tweed jacket with brown trousers tucked into high boots. His hair was straight and sandy. His eyes were small and beady. His nose was long and thin, and his lips, though thin, were hanging loosely. In long-fingered, slender hands he held a gun with a silencer on it. I asked, "Who are you?"

His eyes were drawing an outline of my face and body. "Just call me Josh," he said. "All my friends do."

"I'm not one of your friends," I told him. Then I asked, "You are Joshua Heath?" I remembered what Gail had said about him: "He's a creep." It was an apt description.

"That's right," he said in answer to my question. "I'm a friend of Les Terrell."

"And I'm Judy Carson, his secretary. And I don't think he'd like you pointing a gun at me."

The loose lips formed something that I presumed was supposed to be a smile. "He won't know anything about it," he told me confidentially.

"Where did you come from?" I demanded. Strangely enough, I wasn't afraid of him.

"Oh, I've been here off and on all summer." He was only a few feet from me, and the silencer on the end of the gun was not the pleasantest thing I'd ever seen. I asked, "Does Leslie know you're here now?"

"Sure. I have a standing invitation. Didn't he ever tell you about me? We grew up together over in Indo-China."

"Are your mother and father here?"

"Yes, they're here. They're over at the hotel in Cobleskill."

I remembered the mysterious light in the barn the night before. "You are living in the barn?"

"Sometimes. Sometimes we stay up in the attic here. At present my mother is in the hospital."

"But if you are friends of Leslie's, why don't you stay in one of these apartments, or in one of the guest rooms over at the white house?"

He really smiled then, revealing small uneven yellowish teeth. "A matter of expediency," he explained.

"Then if you are a Heath, it was your folks who sold Leslie this cabinet and that Buddha?"

"That's right."

"Did he know what was in the cabinet?"

"No, of course not."

"Did they?"

"I doubt it. They are very strait-laced."

"Was it you who stole the emeralds from the Buddha's eyes?"

He looked surprised at that. "No." He

glanced over at the Buddha. "My God! They're gone!"

"And you didn't know?"

"No. Where are they?"

"I don't know," I lied.

He suddenly remembered to watch me again and lifted the gun closer to me.

I asked, "Are the police after you?"

He smiled at that. "Not the local police. They're too dumb. I'm an international character. Interpol stuff." He was bragging like a child, and it dawned on me he was "on a trip," as they say. Then perhaps the packages of white powder I was holding in my hands were his. I asked him, "Does this belong to you?"

He said, "Yes, you little snoop." He came close enough to me to grab the powder, and I had to let him have it.

There was the sound of a car stopping at the front door, and, glancing out, I saw it was Leslie's green sedan. I said, "Here's Les."

With a quick movement Josh slipped the white packages into the patch pockets of his jacket and slid the gun under the sofa. By the time Les was out of his car and in the house, he was relaxing on the sofa, smoking a cigarette. I was too speechless to make a sound. I just stood there and stared at him.

Les had a bag of groceries in his arms. When he saw me he said, "Good morning. I had to go down to the village, so I thought I'd bring up some more food." Then he saw Joshua. "Well!" he cried, his face lighting with a welcoming smile. "So you two have met?" He put the bag of groceries on a chair.

Josh said, "Yes. You have good taste."

Les laughed. "I was just lucky this time. You been here long?"

"Since yesterday. I hired a car and left it in the woods and holed up in your barn last night."

Leslie's face sobered. "I thought that was you. I saw the light last night. They after you again?"

Josh looked at his cigarette, and his face was grim, his loose lips tight. "They were asking questions over at the Hunt Club," he said. "Seems they missed a few of their guns."

"I told you to be careful over there."

"I thought I was being careful. And I'll send them the money for their damned guns as soon as I can."

"When do you take off?"

"The helicopter is coming for me tonight. Everything is all packed, in bales of your admirable hay."

"Where are your folks?"

"Dad's in the hotel in Cobleskill, and Mother is in the hospital. She gets that fever every year, and this year it's worse than usual."

"I'm sorry. I'll go over and see her."

"She'd like that."

"Then they won't be going back with you?"

"Not this time."

"Anything I can do?"

"Only shut your eyes to everything."

I couldn't stand it any longer. I just had to know. I asked, "Did you shoot an arrow at me yesterday?"

The loose smile came to his lips. "I shot past you," he said. "I couldn't let you get into the barn. I hadn't finished my packing yet."

He winked at Les, but Les wasn't amused. He said, "We had the police up here yesterday. They searched the barn. If any of those guns had been lying around, I'd have had some explaining to do."

"Oh, there weren't any in sight. The ones that weren't packed were under the floor boards in the hayloft. What do you think I am — a fool?"

Les said, "No." Then he asked, "Was it you who hit me over the head yesterday?"

Josh moved uneasily on the sofa, and

ashes from his cigarette dropped on the floor. "I'm sorry about that, but I thought you were going to phone the police." He smiled with one side of his mouth. "And I couldn't have that. Now could I?"

Les said, "You know I wouldn't do that."

A hard glint came into Joshua's beady eyes. "No, I don't. And I don't trust anybody."

"It seems like you've got to trust me, Josh," Les said patiently, as if he were talking to a child. "After all, you're on my property, and I wouldn't be too popular in this section of the country if it was discovered that I was harboring a gun runner."

Josh made a disparaging noise with his mouth. "Oh, don't give me that holier-than-thou bit. You know perfectly well that if I don't get back with enough guns to start a home guard, the Commies from the north will take over our village."

Les nodded. "Yes, I know," he said.

Josh met his eyes defiantly. "And if that village we used to live in when we were kids had had a home guard and enough guns, maybe your folks wouldn't have been killed."

Les nodded his head, his face grim. "I realize that, too," he said.

Josh got to his feet. "Well, there are still

missionaries and teachers and nurses over there and their lives won't be worth a nickel unless I can get back with those guns."

Les stood up. "I'll drive you over to the barn," he told Josh. To me he said, "You'd better stay here. You don't want to get mixed up with this other racket."

As the two men started out, I couldn't resist saying, "You forgot your gun, Josh."

Both men turned, Les looking surprised and Josh annoyed. But he came back and pulled his gun from beneath the sofa, tossed me a "Thanks," and rejoined Les at the door. I was tempted also to mention the small white packages in his jacket pockets, but decided I'd better not push my luck too far. However, I did say, "Oh, Les, Gail has come back."

"Where is she?"

"She went down to the morgue to identify that girl."

"Does she know who she is?"

"Yes. She's her twin sister."

Les was close to me in two long strides. Grabbing my arms, he said, "Her twin sister?"

I nodded. "Yes. She was mentally deficient and was put in an institution when she was seven."

His hands on my arms tightened. "I don't

believe it. I never heard of her."

"No. Gail says their parents were ashamed of her."

"How did she get here?"

"Gail brought her."

He stared down at me. "But then Aunt Margaret and Uncle Jim must have recognized her yesterday! Why did they say they didn't know who she was?" He was breathing heavily, and his eyes were beginning to hold anger.

"Because they don't want their friends in Westport to know about her."

He let go of me and ran a hand through his already mussed hair. "I can't believe it!" he said. "I can't believe a mother and father could do a thing like that, least of all Aunt Margaret and Uncle Jim."

From the doorway Josh said, "Come on! I haven't much time, and I have a lot to do." If he'd been listening to what we said he gave no indication of being at all interested.

Rather crossly Les said, "Then you'd better go ahead. I have things to do here."

Josh asked, "Are the keys in the car?"

Les said, "Yes. Go on. I'll walk over."

Josh went out and slammed the door, and Les shoved me over to the sofa, pulling me down beside him. "Now tell me what's going on. Why did you come over here?"

"I thought you might be here."

He noticed the open cabinet for the first time. "Who opened that?"

"I did."

"What for?"

"I got to thinking — maybe there was something in there that somebody wanted."

He shook his head in annoyance. "I could have told you there was nothing there. All the drawers are completely empty."

"But they weren't. That one with the lid has a false bottom. My finger touched it accidentally, and it opened, and I found several small white packages containing what must be heroin."

Les jumped up, went to the cabinet, examined the drawer and then swung around to face me. "Where is it?" he demanded.

I hesitated. Could I be sure the information came to him as a surprise? If he'd known the stuff was there, what would he do to me now that I had discovered it? His eyes were angry, his face flushed. I had no choice but to tell him the truth. "Josh has it."

"How did *he* get it?"

"He came in just as I found it, and he pointed that gun at me and then snatched it. He says it's his. He's got it in the pockets of his jacket."

"Stay here!" Les ordered, and strode out of the house.

I practically collapsed against the back of the sofa. Now what? I thought.

I didn't have long to wait. In a few minutes the sound of the motorcycle rent the air, and Roger zoomed to a stop in a cloud of dust. I jumped up and went out to confront him. "Where have you been?" I demanded.

I was furious at him for walking out the day of the murder, but he was unperturbed. Taking off his helmet and wiping the sweat from his forehead, he gave a charming smile. "Well, if it isn't the new secretary," he said.

"Where have you been?" I asked again.

He parked the motorcycle beside the porch and joined me. "Come inside and I'll tell you." He pushed me ahead of him into the living room, pulled me down on the sofa beside him and began kissing me. He smelled of liquor and sweat, and I struggled against him, trying to turn my face so his horrible mouth couldn't touch my lips. But he was stronger than I was. Oh, Les! I thought desperately. Come back and save me! But thoughts do not have the wings we often wish them to have.

So it wasn't Les who saved me, but Gail.

Neither Roger nor I heard her come in. When she said, "So this is the way you mourn your dead wife," Roger jumped up, leaving me lying there on the sofa, breathless from my futile struggle with him.

When he saw Gail, his flushed face paled and his eyes looked as if they would pop right out of his head. *"You!"* he gasped. "But you're dead! I saw you with a knife in your heart!"

"That *you* had put there?" Gail's voice was edged with the bitterness she had every right to feel.

"No! No! I swear it! I didn't kill you."

Then Gail laughed, and the sound of it was so sharp it sent a cold chill through me. "No, you didn't kill me. For as you can see, I am very much alive. And if you don't believe your eyes, maybe you'll believe this." She walked over to him and slapped his face so hard it sounded like a pistol shot.

He stood there staring at her for a moment; then he put a trembling hand up to his cheek, that had almost instantly reddened in the shape of his wife's hand. By that time I had managed to sit up on the sofa and straighten myself out.

Gail turned to me. "So you don't take care of other girls' husbands?" she said scathingly.

"But I didn't." I protested. "He — he —"

"He attacked you?" she said with a sneer. "Oh, sure. I've heard that one before, too. Well, you can have him, if you want. I've had it!" She turned to him, her teeth and hands clenched. "And if you killed my sister, I'll — I'll —" Words failed her, and her eyes were filled with tears.

"Your *sister?*" Roger asked. "Was that girl your sister?"

"Yes, she was."

"But you don't have a sister."

"Oh, yes, I do — had — until you killed her, thinking she was me."

He grabbed her shoulders and shook her. "But I didn't! I didn't kill anybody! You've got to believe me! I *did* think she was *you* when I saw her lying here on the floor with the knife in her heart. Oh, Gail! Oh, my dear!" He grabbed her and hugged her close to him, and in a moment they were both crying like a couple of children, sobbing and hugging each other frantically until I felt a lump come into my throat and tears come to my eyes. There are many kinds of love, and this was a brand I had never seen before — a love-hate that was frightening.

I got up off the sofa and went into the bedroom I had used the first night. There wasn't any door, so I couldn't shut myself off, but I could go into the bathroom and close the door. Only there wasn't anything I could do in there, because I didn't have my toilet articles. After a while I heard Roger and Gail go upstairs, so I came out of the bathroom and went into the living room. If I'd had the galleys and the notebook, I could have worked, but they were over at the white house. So I wandered around the room aimlessly.

As I passed the cabinet, I closed all the drawers and the doors at the front, wishing I had minded my own business and not deliberately looked for trouble. Then I went over to the Buddha. She had such a smug, enigmatic look that I became angry with her, which, of course, was foolish. I reached out a hand and began feeling of her. She was smooth and cool to the touch. I put a finger in the empty eye sockets. In the right one there was a small, slightly raised spot. I pushed at it and to my amazement a drawer at the base of the statute began to open slowly. I stood there watching it, and suddenly I began to tremble. In the drawer were at least a dozen uncut diamonds and emeralds. So this was why the eyes had been taken out of the statue! Someone knew that the only way to release the secret drawer was to press that tiny raised spot in the socket of the right eye, and to do that the emerald eyes had to be taken out.

So *now* what should I do? Close the drawer and say nothing about it? Call Leslie and tell him to come right over? But if he was out in the barn with Josh, he wouldn't hear the phone.

I wondered if Josh knew about the secret drawer. Had his parents known when they had sold the Buddha to Leslie? Or was it a plot in which Leslie himself was involved? What did I know about him? Nothing, actually. He could be the biggest crook in the world, for all I knew. Lots of crooks were charming, well educated, from good backgrounds.

I decided to close the drawer and keep the knowledge of it to myself. If anyone knew of the drawer and its contents, let him do whatever he wanted to do about it. It was none of my business. I turned and walked away from the Buddha, and as I did so I had the feeling that her sightless eyes were watching me.

From upstairs came the sound of Gail and Roger singing one of their folk songs and the twang of the guitar. It was a mournful sound, and I wanted to get away from it. I picked up the bag of groceries Leslie had left on the chair and carried it out to the kitchen. He hadn't said whether the food was for me or for himself. Well, if it didn't have refrigeration soon, it would begin to spoil, for it was another hot day. When I had everything put away, I decided I was hungry, so I fixed myself some lunch and sat down at a table by a window to eat it. The back garden was very pretty in the bright sunlight, and the usual bees and yellow jackets were hovering over the sweetest of the flowers, making a gentle humming sound that was soothing.

When I finished eating and returned to the living room, everything was quiet upstairs. I picked up a magazine and sat down to read, but I couldn't keep my mind on it. About three o'clock in the afternoon, Leslie drove over with my bags. "You'd better stay here tonight," he said when he brought them in.

I said, "Oh, no! I can't. I don't want to!"

"Then you'll have to go over to the hotel. I don't want you over at my place tonight." Then he asked, "Why don't you want to stay here?"

"That's a stupid question, after what has happened here. But in addition to that, Gail and Roger are upstairs, and I don't want to stay here with them."

"They're *both* here?" he asked, his eyes

wide with astonishment.

"Yes."

"Where have they been?"

"I don't know."

"Well, I'm jolly well going to find out!" He turned to go upstairs, but I stopped him. "Don't go up now. They have some things to straighten out between them."

He stopped and came over to me. "And neither of them said where they'd been?"

"No. And Roger didn't know Gail had a sister."

He chewed at his upper lip and ran a hand through his hair. "Blast it!" he said explosively. "How did things get into such a mess?"

"I wouldn't know. I just work here. And incidentally, did you bring over the galleys and my notebook so I can work?"

"No, I never thought about them."

"Have you heard anything more about the inquest?"

"Oh, yes, I forgot to tell you. I stopped in the police station when I went to the village. The inquest is set for eleven o'clock the day after tomorrow."

"Will Gail and Roger have to appear?"

"I should think so."

"Do you think they will?"

Les shrugged. "If they don't, they're apt to be arrested."

"On what grounds?"

He smiled slightly. "That's a good question." He came and sat down beside me on the sofa. Then he glanced over at the cabinet. "Did you close it?" he asked.

"Yes."

"I made Josh give me those packages."

"And he did it without a fight?"

"Oh, yes. How many were there?"

"Six."

"The son of a b— he only gave me four."

"Then he still has a good supply."

"Oh, well, he'll probably sell it to help pay for the guns he's been salvaging."

"From where?"

"Oh, sporting goods stores, pawn shops, the Hunt Club. Anywhere he could find them."

"What will happen to him if he's caught before he gets out of the country?"

Les shrugged. "He'll be arrested. But he'll make it all right. There is a private helicopter picking him up tonight. They will land in that field near the barn and take him and his bales of hay to a tramp steamer that is docked down in the Hudson on the Jersey shore. The cargo will be listed as alfalfa for an underdeveloped country."

"If he should be caught, what about you?"

"If they could prove I helped him, I'd be an accessory, I suppose."

"And you are willing to take the chance?"

"If it will save the lives of people like my parents who are over in a foreign country trying to help — missionaries, teachers, nurses. They're doing a magnificent job and getting no credit at all."

"But shouldn't the government take care of them?"

"Theoretically. But there could be a lot of dead people before the government red tape got untangled. Look at Vietnam."

"When the Heaths sold you that Buddha and the cabinet, do you think they knew there was anything hidden in them?"

He shook his head. "No, I'm sure they didn't."

"Did Josh, do you think?"

"Possibly. Josh is a strange mixture of good and bad."

I got up and walked over to the Buddha. "Come here. I want to show you something."

He got up and came over, and I took his right hand, singled out the index finger and put the tip of it on the small raised spot in the socket of the Buddha's right eye. "Push," I said.

He looked down at me inquiringly.

"Go on, push," I told him.

He did, and slowly the secret drawer at the bottom of the Buddha began to open. When he saw the diamonds and emeralds, he drew in a sharp breath. "Good God!" he said in a whisper.

I looked up at him. "Who do you suppose put them there?"

"I haven't the remotest conception."

"Joshua?"

"Could be. He does strange things. If he did, he stole them from somewhere."

"Did he come over to this country when his parents came and brought the furniture?"

"Yes. This spring."

"If he knows the gems are here, he isn't apt to leave tonight without them."

"I wouldn't think so."

"What are you going to do?"

Les shoved the drawer shut. "Nothing," he said.

I felt myself getting angry. "But you can't be so passive!" I cried.

He patted my shoulder. "Take it easy," he cautioned. "It isn't your problem."

"You're right. It isn't. But I sure landed in the middle of it with both feet."

He thought a moment, then asked,

"Didn't either Gail or Roger say where they'd been?"

"No."

"Didn't you ask them?"

"Of course."

"And what did they say?"

"Gail told me it was none of my business. But she said if *you* asked her she would tell you, because it was partly your business."

A worried look came into his eyes. "I wonder —" he mused. Then he asked, "And what did Roger say?"

I hesitated. I didn't want to tell him about Roger making love to me — or trying to. I said, "He avoided giving me an answer."

"Were Gail and Roger together — wherever they were?"

"No, I'm sure they weren't, because Roger thought Gail was dead. He thought that girl was his wife."

"Wasn't he shocked when he saw her alive?"

"Yes."

"Has Gail called her folks?"

"Not as far as I know. I told her she should, and she said if they had deliberately repudiated Carol — that's her sister's name — then she didn't ever want to have anything to do with them again."

Les raised his eyebrows. "Can't say I

blame her. It was a pretty lousy thing to do."

"But they will all have to meet at the inquest, won't they?"

"If Roger and Gail stay around long enough to go."

"Shouldn't the police be told they have returned?"

"Eventually."

"You don't think the police might be watching us?"

"I doubt it. Besides, if Gail went down to the morgue, then they know she is here and alive."

"When you went to the police station this morning, didn't they tell you she'd been there?"

"I went early, before she'd been there."

"I suppose to tell them you'd take care of things?" "Yes."

"I told Gail you'd said you were going to."

"What did she say?"

"That it was just the kind of a thing you would do." He smiled ruefully.

"Are you going to call her mother?"

"No. But I'll insist Gail call her."

"Suppose she refuses?"

"Then they will meet at the inquest."

"If Gail and Roger attend the inquest."

"Gail didn't say whether or not the police

had questioned her?"

"No."

"It stands to reason they must have."

"You'd think so. Are you going to help Josh finish his packing?"

"If I see he isn't going to get through in time. I want him and his contraband off the property tonight."

"When did Gail ever meet him?"

He showed surprise at my question. "A couple of times this spring while the Heaths were using this apartment. The three of them were in the apartment, and Gail and Roger came up for a couple of days. Why?"

I couldn't suppress a smile. "She says he's a creep."

Les laughed. "I suppose a girl *would* feel that way about him. I guess I'm just used to him. We were like brothers when we were kids."

"What are his parents like?"

"Oh, they are very kindly people. They were always very good to me after I lost my own folks and went to live with them. They were strict with Josh and me. Wouldn't stand for any nonsense. We had to go to school and do our lessons and go to church and Sunday school and take part in the activities of the missionaries, and help out in any way we could."

"Do they know what Josh is doing? About the guns?"

"No, I'm sure they don't."

"If they knew, would they let him do it?"

"I don't see how they could stop him. He's a big boy now."

"Does he do anything for a living? I mean over in Indo-China?"

"Yes. He teaches in the American school there in their village."

There were sounds of movement upstairs, and Gail and Roger came thumping, down the stairs and into the living room. When Gail saw Les, she said, "Hi."

He got to his feet. "Where were you?" he asked her.

"Where you told me to go. To see my doctor in the city."

"Then you've been down in your apartment?"

"No. I was in the hospital for tests."

Leslie's broad shoulders seemed to droop. "And?" he asked.

"Negative, just as you told me." But she avoided his eyes as she spoke, and I had the feeling she was lying.

Les gave a sigh of relief and turned to Roger, who was lighting a cigarette. "And where did *you* go yesterday?" he demanded.

Roger walked over to a large easy chair, sank down on it and stretched out his long legs.

"I went down to the city and stayed with a friend. I didn't want to get mixed up in the mess here."

"Even though you thought the murdered girl was your wife?"

He looked down at the lighted end of his cigarette. "I had things to do in the city," he said.

Gail went over and stood in front of him. "Tell him," she said. "Tell him you went down to visit my lawyer to see if you could find out how much money I'd left you in my will."

Roger looked up at her and grinned. "Any law against that?" he asked.

"None whatever. But you didn't find out, did you?"

He shrugged. "So? You didn't die, did you?"

"So you came back up here to play the heartbroken husband."

He got to his feet and pushed her aside so he could walk across the room to the Buddha. "Oh, come off it," he said petulantly. "I thought we straightened that all out upstairs."

"Just because you made love to me?"

Gail's blue-green eyes were flashing danger signals.

He whirled around and glared at her. "You liked it, didn't you?"

Her chin went up, and her hands clenched at her sides. "Yes, I liked it," she admitted, "because I'm fool enough to love you. Don't ask me why, because I don't know."

"It's just my overwhelming charm." Roger grinned.

Les said, "Okay, kids; cut it out. If you've kissed and made up, why don't you let it go at that?" Then he asked, "Have you called your mother, Gail?"

"No, and I'm not going to. If she wouldn't claim Carol's body, I don't ever want to see her again."

"But you are going to have to, the day after tomorrow at the inquest."

Wearily she said, "I know. They told me down at the police station."

Leslie's lips tightened, and he spoke like a stern father. "And don't either of you do any more disappearing acts between now and then. If you do, I'll send a posse after you."

"But we have engagements," Roger protested. "We're supposed to be at the Concord Hotel tomorrow for a week."

"You'll have to cancel."

"But we can't. We need the money."

Gail drew in a heavy breath. "Oh shut up!" she told her husband. Surprisingly, he did just that. He shrugged and sauntered over to a window and stood there looking out with his back to the room.

Gail asked Les, "Is that creep Joshua Heath here again? I thought I saw him wandering around the barn."

"Yes, he's here. And if you meet up with him, I'll thank you to be civil to him."

"Then tell him to keep his hands off me."

"What do you mean by that?"

Gail tossed back her long blonde hair impatiently. "Oh, for heaven's sakes!" she cried. "What do you think I mean? Those mealy-mouthed missionaries are just like everybody else." She turned to me. "Just don't let yourself be caught alone in the same room with him," she warned me.

I had to smile. "I've already had that experience," I told her.

"Then you know what I mean?"

"I have a good imagination, but my experience with him was more frightening. You see, he pointed a gun at me."

"No kidding?" Gail smiled.

Les said, "Suppose we all have dinner here tonight? Judy and I will get it."

Chapter Eight

Our dinner wasn't exactly a success. Les and I did all the work, and Gail and Roger condescended to eat the food. Les tried to keep an amicable conversation going, but it was hopeless. Gail and Roger just sulked, and Gail didn't actually eat much. While Les and I were working in the kitchen together, I asked, "What about Joshua's dinner?"

"He'll go into the house and get himself something."

"How many bales of hay is he taking?"

"About two dozen."

"Will they all go on the helicopter?"

"They will have to make two trips, maybe three. They have a large trailer truck hidden somewhere near an open field where the helicopter can land, and the truck will transport the stuff to the ship."

"But if the bales of hay are going as alfalfa to an underprivileged country, wouldn't there be more of it sent? Say a boatload, at least?"

"Not necessarily. It will be a private contribution from a few interested people, like a church sending a few boxes of old clothes to the missions."

"I see."

Shortly after dinner, Les said, "Well, I guess I'll go on home. You folks will be all right here."

Neither Gail nor Roger answered. I said, "I hope," and Gail gave me a quick look.

After Les left, Gail and Roger went up to their own apartment, and I stayed in the living room trying to read magazines. But I couldn't keep my mind from the jewels in the secret compartment of the Buddha. Would Josh leave without them, possibly leave them for another trip back to the States? Or didn't he even know they were there?

About ten o'clock I went to bed, putting out all the living room lights and locking both the front and back doors. There were still lights on in the white house, but no sign of a light in the barn. I fervently hoped that Josh would get away all right without any trouble. Whether what he was doing was right or wrong was none of my business. I suppose if I had known any of those missionaries, teachers or nurses personally, I would have wanted them to have guns to protect themselves.

I must have slept several hours before I was awakened by the sound of the helicopter. I sat up in bed and looked at the clock. It was three A.M. I wondered if this was the first, second or third trip for the helicopter. I could easily have slept through the first and second. There was no sound from the apartment upstairs, and I couldn't resist getting up, putting on my slippers and negligee and going into the living room. All was quiet in there.

Suddenly I wanted Les, wanted him desperately, wanted to feel his arms around me, his lips on mine.

I was deep in my sentimental dream, curled up on the sofa, when I began to have the feeling I was not alone in the room. I might even have dozed off for a moment, but now I was wide awake.

Standing in the middle of the room was a shadowy figure, and it was moaning softly to itself, "Hans, Hans, Hans."

I spoke to it. "Singing Bird?" I asked. Strangely enough, I wasn't frightened. If this was a ghost, it couldn't possibly hurt me.

"Hans," the figure whispered. It was coming toward me and holding out its arms. As my eyes became accustomed to the darkness, I could see the iridescent glow of the skeletal hands, like the one I had seen that first night, and the face also had an iridescent glow of blue, green and red. The hands were reaching for my throat, and I screamed, suddenly afraid. Then something hit me on the back of the head, and the next thing I knew I sneezed and discovered I was lying on some hay and there was a rag in my mouth and another around the lower part of my face, tied at the back of my head so I couldn't cry out. I could hear movement around me but no voices. Looking up, I could just barely distinguish beams overhead. Where was I? In the barn? Who had carried me there? Josh? I shuddered to think he had handled me when I had nothing on but a nightdress and a thin negligee. I wondered where Les was. I couldn't call out, and when I tried to sit up I discovered my ankles were tied together, and my hands were tied behind my back and were numb from the weight of my body. And I was very frightened.

Then I heard a match strike and saw something that looked like the lighted end of a cigarette. A man's voice said, "Put that out, you fool! Do you want to set the place on fire?"

Another voice said, "I'll be careful. There are only a couple more to go; then we can get away. What are you going to do with the girl?"

"Take her with us."

"In a bale of hay?"

"Sure. That way no one will know we have her."

"She'll smother."

"No, she won't. I'll pack her carefully." Josh chuckled at the idea.

The other voice said, "You darn fool! Can't you keep your hands off women? You killed that one the other night, and now you'll kill this one. Isn't gun-running enough for you to get caught on? Do you want to get sent up for murder, too?"

So Josh had killed Carol. He had probably been trying to make love to her, thinking she was Gail. He said, "I won't be if you keep your mouth shut. And I wouldn't have killed that girl over at the brick house if she hadn't put up a fight when I tried to kiss her."

My heart began to pound with fright, and I struggled to sit up. I made as much noise as I could in my throat, but it wasn't loud enough to be heard.

I wondered where Les was. Neither of the voices had belonged to him. The first one had been Josh, of that I was sure. The other could be the pilot of the helicopter. And if Les was in the house keeping out of the way until the last bale of hay was air-borne, it would be too late by the time he discovered I was missing.

A man came over to the bale of hay I was lying on, and I struggled violently so he couldn't help but notice. He said, "Oh, so you're all right?" It was Josh.

I made an angry sound in my throat to indicate I wasn't all right. But he took no notice; just began to put hay over me. He said, "Don't worry. I'll leave you enough air to breathe, but I'll have to tie you to the bale so you won't fall out."

I squirmed and made guttural sounds in my throat, but he just said, "Keep still. You won't get hurt if you just take it easy."

But I couldn't keep still. I was too terrified. My face was now covered with the hay. It tickled my nose, and I began to sneeze. That is, I did what I could to sneeze with that horrid rag stuffed in my mouth and the other tied over it.

Then I wobbled about as Josh began to tie rope around the bale of hay. Oh, Les! I prayed. Please help me! But there was no help forthcoming, and Josh called, "Hey Pete, help me carry this out to the copter." The next thing I knew, the bale of hay I was lying in was lifted and carried. Outside of the barn, I could feel more air filtering through the hay that was covering me so I could breathe better, but I knew I would surely suffocate before I was released.

There must have been portable stairs from the ground up to the door of the helicopter, because the bale of hay was tilted as the two men carried it up the steps. Then it was dropped down, and I heard Josh say, "Put it over here. If it gets mixed up with the others and gets turned over, or one of the others falls on top of it, she'll smother."

The man called Pete just grunted, and in a moment the bale I was in was put down on a solid surface. Josh said, "All right; that's it. We can take off now. Pull up the steps."

Then, like a miracle, I heard a shout. It was Leslie's voice. "Hey! Wait a minute!" he called.

Josh yelled, "What do you want?"

"You've set the barn on fire!" Les yelled. "Come and help me put it out!"

"We can't. We haven't time!"

"Don't give me that!" Les yelled, and I could hear his feet running up the steps to the copter. Then I heard him cry, "What are you doing? I'm not going with you!"

"You are now," Josh said. Then to Pete, "Close her up and get going." There was the sound of a struggle, then the noise of the steps being pulled up and the door being slammed shut, then the revving of the motor and the whirr of the propellers.

Les must have chosen my bale of hay to sit or fall on in his struggle with Josh, because his whole weight landed on me. I squirmed and began making as much noise in my throat as I could. I realized that with the noise of the whirring propellers and the engine, he wouldn't be able to hear me. But surely he must be able to feel me beneath him and realize that guns wouldn't be moving around the way I was doing.

I could feel the helicopter taking off, and I squirmed around frantically. Then the weight of Leslie's body lifted, and the hay covering me was being taken away, and hands were pulling me up. There was light in the helicopter, and when the hay was taken off me Les could see what it was that had been squirming around beneath him. Josh and Pete were both up front in the cockpit, and Les and I and the bales of hay were alone in what I guess you'd call the cabin, which had had the seats removed.

When Les saw the way I was tied, he quickly released me, took the horrid rags from my face and mouth, then gathered me into his arms and held me close without asking any questions. I couldn't even cry. I just clung to him and trembled.

We were near a window, and I could see a

red glow in the darkness of the night. Les swore. Looking out, I saw the barn below us, now burning like a bright bonfire. I pulled away from him, crying, "Oh, how awful! Can't we do something?"

Les said, "Too late now to save the barn. I just hope there isn't enough wind to blow it toward the house."

"And your lab."

"Yes."

The helicopter was circling over the barn as if Josh and Pete were enjoying the sight of the fire.

Then Les surprised me by taking a gun out of his pocket — the one I'd seen in the kitchen drawer. He went forward to the cockpit and, holding the gun to Pete's head, apparently ordered him to take the helicopter down. Josh tried to knock the gun from Leslie's hand, but Les pushed him back into his seat. In another moment the helicopter was making wider circles and eventually came to a landing in a field far enough away from the burning barn not to be affected by the fire. With the engine shut off and the propellers slowing to a halt, it was possible for voices to be heard without shouting.

Les ordered, "Now! Open the door and put down the steps, and then you two rats go down first. I'll be right behind you, so don't try anything."

The two men did as they were told; Les was close behind them. To me he said, "You follow me, and go into the house and phone for the fire department."

"Will they come way up here?"

"Yes. But they won't be able to save the barn. And then call the police and tell them to come up."

"But I thought you didn't want them to know."

"Don't argue! Do as I tell you!"

Meekly I said, "Yes, Mr. Terrell." I wondered what he was going to do with Josh and Pete, but I didn't have long to find out. He herded them ahead of him toward the house, which was uphill from the field in which the helicopter had landed, saying to me, "You'd better run, if you can."

"I can." And I did.

By the time Les arrived with his hostages, I'd alerted the fire department. I told the man who answered the phone that the barn was on fire up on the mountain and asked him also to bring the police.

He asked, "What do you want the police for?"

I said, "Please don't waste time asking questions! Just hurry and bring the police."

He said, "All right, lady. Take it easy."

The crackling of the burning barn sounded loud in the quiet of the night, and sparks were flying toward the starlit heavens. Fortunately, the wind was relatively calm, and what little there was was blowing away from the house so there was a chance it would escape damage.

Looking over to the brick house, I saw lights on the first floor, in the living room. If Gail and Roger saw the fire, they would surely come over — to look if not to help.

Les had Josh and Pete backed up against the house now and was guarding them with the pistol at the ready. Josh was giving him an argument, but all Les said was, "Shut up!"

After a few minutes we heard the fire whistle blowing down in the village, and in a few minutes the wail of the truck sirens coming up the mountain road. There was also the wail of the police siren. Josh said, "You darn fool! You've ruined everything!"

But again all Les said was, "Shut up!" And when the police and firemen arrived, he put away his gun, telling Josh and Pete, "Don't try any tricks or you'll be sorry."

The two of them just glared at him; I'm sure they both would have enjoyed killing him.

From then on all the men worked to put out the fire and keep it from spreading. Even Josh and Pete worked. I knew they hadn't deliberately set the fire. It had been caused by a spark from Pete's cigarette, and they probably felt sorry about it.

The police didn't ask why they'd been sent for; they just did what they could to help. I guess the police always accompany the fire department on a call, anyway. And only one patrol car containing two policemen came.

I was told to keep out of the way, and I realized that by doing as I was told I was helping in the only way I could.

I watched to see if Gail and Roger would come over, but they didn't. This puzzled me. Had they left again without saying goodbye? I knew that going off and leaving lights on in the house would be the least of their concerns.

It was early dawn by the time the fire was put out, leaving the barn nothing but a smoldering ruin. But at least the house had been saved. Leslie thanked the firemen and the two policemen, and let them leave without telling them anything about Josh and Pete. Surprisingly enough, no one seemed to notice the helicopter, I guess because it was set down in the field, which was lower than the house and barn.

When the firemen and police had gone, Les shook hands with Josh and Pete, saying, "Sorry I had to detain you. I hope you haven't missed your boat."

Josh said, "If we have, we'll be back."

Quietly Les said, "I wouldn't if I were you. There will be no place to hide out now the barn is gone. And there isn't any more hay."

I wanted to ask Josh if he'd taken the jewels from the Buddha after he'd knocked me over the head, but decided I'd keep out of it. I was only too glad to be alive. Neither Josh nor Pete included me in their good-byes. They just turned and walked away toward the helicopter, and Les let them go.

As soon as they were out of sight, I asked Les, "Now *why* did you let them go?"

He grinned. "I had to let them accomplish their mission," he said. "If they miss that tramp steamer, it will be a long time before there is space available on another with a captain they can trust."

"But Josh was kidnaping me!"

"Couldn't blame him for that. You're a darned pretty girl."

"But he might have killed me!"

His face sobered at that. "Yes, he might have. Thank heaven the barn caught fire.

Otherwise I'd never have known you were on the helicopter. And now we'd better get to bed and get some sleep."

I asked, "Do you think Josh took the jewels from the secret drawer in the Buddha?"

"I don't know and I don't care. He probably stole them from somewhere in Indo-China and hid them in the Buddha to get them over here, so let him have them. Besides, I'm fed up with the whole business. Now I'll drive you over to the brick house."

"But I don't want to go back there ever again."

He took hold of my arm and began to walk around to his car. "Oh, don't be that way!" he said crossly. "All your things are over there. You might as well finish the night there."

I pulled away from him and stood directly in front of him so he had to stop walking. Looking up at him, I demanded, "Don't you want to know how I got on that helicopter, bound and gagged and stuffed into a bale of hay like a gun?"

"Can't you tell me that in the morning?"

"But it could have been the end of me!"

He sighed and patted my cheek with a gentle hand. "I know. But it wasn't."

"And you don't think Josh should be arrested for kidnaping and attempted murder?"

"Not this time. Besides, his life won't be too safe when he gets back to that little village in Indo-China, even with all his guns. At least give him a fighting chance."

"Then if you're such a good friend of his, why did you let him go?"

Les ran a hand through his tousled hair, which I noticed was slightly singed in several places from too close contact with the fire. "Because that was what he wanted to do." He took hold of my arm again and said, "Come on, let's go. I'm tired and want to get to bed."

I also was tired, too tired to argue any more. If the ghost of Singing Bird was still over at the brick house waiting to strangle me with her skeletal iridescent hands, I didn't much care.

In the car, Les said, "Gail and Roger must be up. The lights are on downstairs."

I said, "Yes, I guess so. Wouldn't you have thought they'd have come over when they saw the fire? They must have seen it."

"Nothing *they* do or don't do surprises me. They're a couple of weirdos."

"They sure are. If I may say so, all of your friends and relatives seem to be a bit weird."

He smiled at that. "You can say that

again." Then he patted my knee. "Except you."

I moved away from him. "I'm neither a friend nor a relative," I told him.

He sighed. "That's right. You're not."

In the east, the grayness of the sky was gradually becoming brighter, and a rosy hue began to spread across the horizon. The sun, looking like a piece of orange-red plastic that was being pushed up from behind the distant mountain, seemed to have no form, no brilliance. And its rays had not yet penetrated through the earth's atmosphere. I drew in a deep breath of the clean early morning air. "For a while last night," I said, "I didn't think I'd ever see that again."

"What?"

"The sun."

"Oh, yes. I guess it was a rather harrowing experience."

"It was all of that."

We had reached the brick house by then, and Les stopped the car. Then, turning to me, he said, "I don't want you to think that I wasn't disturbed by what happened to you last night. It was a dastardly thing for Josh to do, but —" He smiled ruefully. "As they say, all's well that ends well."

I didn't answer him, because suddenly

there was a large lump in my throat, and my eyes were full of tears. I opened the car door and got out. Les said, "Good night. Or I guess it's good morning."

I just nodded and went into the house, through the entrance hall and to the door of the living room. Then I screamed and ran back outside. Les was just turning the car around and hadn't picked up any speed, so I was able to catch him. Screaming and waving my arms frantically, I ran in front of the car, and he had to jam on the brakes to keep from running me down. He jumped out of the car, grabbed me by the shoulders and shook me. "Stop it!" he said crossly. "Stop it and shut up! What's the matter now?"

All I could do was sob and point to the house. With an arm around my trembling shoulders, he led me inside.

The sight that greeted our eyes when we went into the house wasn't pretty. In the living room, lying on the sofa and wearing a long white negligee, her face and hands covered with carbon black and sprinkled with the liquid crystals, was Gail. There was a knife in her heart. And sitting cross-legged on the floor beside her was Roger, strumming on the guitar and crooning a mournful song. Blood from the wound in Gail's chest was slowly dripping down onto Roger's hand as it plucked at the strings of the guitar. The secret drawer to the Buddha was open, and the jewels were gone.

Beside me Les said, "My God!" and ran over to the sofa. Flinging Roger out of the way so he fell sideways on the floor, he bent over Gail, felt of her pulse, and lifted one closed eyelid — the right one with the small red spot on it. Then he gently closed it again, shuddered and turned away.

Roger was getting to his feet. He seemed dazed, hardly conscious of his surroundings. He was holding the neck of the guitar in his bloodstained hand.

Les grabbed a handful of his turtleneck shirt, along with the strings of love beads, and shook him so hard his shaggy head wobbled back and forth. "What did you kill her for?" he asked Roger through clenched teeth.

Roger struck at him with the guitar and wrenched himself free. "I didn't!" he sobbed. "She killed herself. Honest!"

"Don't give me that!" Les told him.

Roger began to shake his head back and forth, and there was a helpless, scared look in his pale blue eyes. "I didn't! I didn't! She did it herself. She told me this afternoon she had cancer and didn't want to live."

"You lie!" Les snapped. "She told me she'd been to the hospital for tests and they were negative."

Roger kept shaking his head back and forth. "She lied to you. She didn't want you to know. And she was pregnant. She didn't want to bring a child into the world — the way she was." Roger was swaying on his feet and looked as if he were going to collapse, and before I could get to him he did, dropping down on his knees and hugging the guitar to his breast as if it were a baby.

Les turned and looked down at Gail. "Where did she get the carbon black and the crystals?" he asked.

"From your lab. She wanted to frighten her." He nodded toward me. "She didn't want her up here because she was afraid you'd fall in love with her." Then it must have been Gail's skeletal hand I'd seen that first night.

I felt my face flush, but Les didn't look at me. He stood looking down at Gail. "Poor kid," he said softly. "Poor kid." Then, without turning, he asked Roger, "Who killed her sister?"

I said, "Josh did. He thought she was Gail and tried to make love to her. She fought him, and he lost his head and killed her. I heard him telling Pete about it in the barn when I was tied up and they didn't know I was conscious."

"And the emerald eyes of the Buddha?" Les asked.

Roger said, "Gail took them. She wanted money to pay our debts. We are pretty deep in the hole. Then she felt guilty and gave them to Josh for some project of his."

"Then how did they get on Carol's eyelids?"

Roger shrugged. "Josh must have put them there. You know him. He's a creep."

Les turned and looked down at him. There was utter contempt on his white, tight face. "She thought you didn't want her to have children," he said. His hands were clenched at his sides, but I could see they were trembling.

Roger shook his head. "I didn't. And it wasn't mine. It was Joshua's. She was furious because he was going back to Indo-China and leaving her."

"She told you all this?"

"Yes."

"When?"

"Tonight. Last night. While your barn was burning."

"Then you saw the fire?"

Roger nodded.

At that point I had to say, "But she told

me she thought Josh was a creep."

"She did. But — it happened in the spring. She was mad at me, as usual, and she wanted to punish me. And she couldn't let a man alone, even if he was a creep."

Les sighed, and his broad shoulders drooped. "Poor mixed-up kid," he said, and went over to a chair, sank down upon it and covered his face with his hands.

I didn't know what to do. I just stood there, looking from Les to Roger and then to the corpse of Gail, lying so still. Then I walked over to the table-desk and picked up the phone and called the police. No one made any attempt to stop me. I had the feeling that neither of the men even so much as heard me.

Chapter Nine

The next couple of weeks were hectic. The Wakefields were prostrate over the loss of Gail. The police questioned them together and separately, but I was not present during any of the sessions.

Roger was held as a material witness, and I think he really felt badly about Gail. In his own peculiar way he had loved her.

Les was questioned extensively, as was I, but neither of us was held.

There was, of course, an investigation as to the cause of the fire by the insurance company, who eventually put down the cause as accidental. Nothing was ever discovered about the guns. Apparently the Hunt Club never made a big thing about their loss.

When it was all over, both girls buried in Westport in the Wakefield family plot, and Roger released after the inquests because of lack of evidence, Les and I were left alone on the mountain top.

It was still a beautiful place to be scenically, and I liked being there. I also liked Leslie, although the fact that he had let

Joshua get away still bothered me. But we never spoke of it, and with his experiments in the lab ruined because he had had to neglect them for so long, he decided to close both houses and return to the city.

He insisted I take my full salary for every day I had been there, even though I had done very little actual work as his secretary.

The day before we were to leave for New York, he said, "I'm going to drive over to the hospital to see Mrs. Heath. Want to come?"

I said, "Yes, I'd like to meet her."

When we went into the room where Mrs. Heath was lying in a bed by a window, with her eyes closed, a tall, thin, elderly man who had been sitting beside her rose to his feet. "Why, hello, Les," he said. "I hoped you'd come before you went back to the city."

Les went over and gripped his hand. "Hello, Uncle John," he said. "How is she?"

The elderly man shook his head, and tears came to his eyes.

Les turned and, leaning over the bed, kissed the woman's cheek. "It's me, Aunt Ida," he said. "Les."

She opened her eyes, and a faint smile fluttered her pale lips. Her face was chalk-white and looked as brittle as parchment. "Josh," she murmured. "Is he all right?"

Les said, "Yes, he's on his way back."

She sighed. "I knew you'd take care of him. Don't ever let anything happen to him, will you?" Her pale, almost sightless eyes looked up at Leslie appealingly.

Les took her frail hand in his. "You know I won't, Aunt Ida," he told her. He leaned down and kissed her forehead, and when he straightened up there were tears in his eyes. Hers were closed again, but there was a smile of peace on her lips.

Les turned to the man. "Josh is all right," he told him. "He sailed a couple of weeks ago."

The man nodded and sat down beside his wife again. There seemed to be no reason to introduce me, so I just stood by silently, but my heart was very full.

On the way back to our mountain top, I said to Les, "That is why you let Josh go. Because of them."

He nodded. "Yes," he said. I didn't ask any more questions, but I felt much better. His passivity had bothered me and had lessened my respect for him, but now that I knew the reason, he looked ten feet tall to me.

During our last breakfast together in the white house before driving back to the city, he said, "I'm sorry you had to have such an unpleasant experience up here on top of my mountain, but outside of all the unpleasant things that have happened, I have enjoyed having you."

I said, "Thank you. And in many ways I've enjoyed being here."

For answer he passed me the plate of hot toast, which was covered with a paper napkin to keep it reasonably warm. "I'm going to need help on that plastics book when I get back to the city," he said.

I smiled as I took a piece of toast. "I'd be glad to help," I told him. "Perhaps I could do it evenings and weekends, if I got another regular job in the daytime, and then you wouldn't have to pay me. I'd enjoy helping."

"I'd appreciate that," he said, looking across the table at me with the old twinkle in his eyes. "And later, when the leaves begin to turn, we could drive up here for weekends."

I hesitated. "Oh, I'm afraid I couldn't do that," I said, and bit into the piece of toast.

"Why not?"

I felt my face flushing and knew I must look like an adolescent schoolgirl. "Oh, I don't know. I'd feel funny deliberately coming up here with you for a weekend."

He tilted back his head and laughed. "You're kidding!"

"No, I'm not. Being here as your secretary was — well, it seemed legitimate, and as things turned out, we haven't been alone much. But to come up for a weekend — just the two of us —"

He was drinking his coffee and almost choked on it. Putting the cup down, he wiped his mouth with his paper napkin, balled it and then threw it down. Then he got up and came around the table. "Get up," he ordered me.

I looked up at him but didn't move. "Come on, get up!" he said.

I got up, and we stood face to face, although I had to tilt mine back so I could look up into his eyes. "I have a surprise for you," he told me.

"What?"

"I no longer want you as a secretary. I'd rather have you as my wife."

I drew in my breath and felt myself start to tremble, and he began to smile. "You wouldn't object to coming up here weekends with your husband, would you?"

I shook my head, and tears came to my eyes. We reached out simultaneously, and our arms went around each other. When he'd finished kissing me, he said, "You little goose."

We kissed again; then I said, "Will you

give me something for a wedding present?"

"Anything you want."

"May I have Yaksa?"

He looked surprised, then began to chuckle. "What on earth for?"

"To pray to. Just to be sure. This mountain top would be such a nice place for children."

He hugged me close to him. "She's yours," he said in my ear. "But I can assure you she won't be needed except as an ornament in the living room."

The employees of Thorndike Press hope you have enjoyed this Large Print book. All our Large Print titles are designed for easy reading, and all our books are made to last. Other Thorndike Press Large Print books are available at your library, through selected bookstores, or directly from us.

For information about titles, please call:

(800) 257-5157

To share your comments, please write:

Publisher
Thorndike Press
P.O. Box 159
Thorndike, Maine 04986